WEST OF THE WARLOCK

Written by
Martin T. Ingham

Published by

Martinus
PUBLISHING

www.martinus.us

This book is dedicated to the American pioneers who struggled to bring civilization to the wild frontier. Without their hard work and determination, their descendants would not be able to weave such wildly exaggerated and mythical tales about their exploits.

Foreword

It was just a little over two years ago that I first began work on West of the Warlock, a book that has become one of my most successful works of fiction. Of course, I tell the story of this book's creation more thoroughly in the original afterword, so I won't waste a lot of time retelling the same old story here. This novel concept was a good one, and I ran with it (and then some). Yet, as I'm deep in the middle of writing the 4th book in the series, I find myself tasked with the perilous and costly job of founding a new publishing company and restoring a 1954 Chevy Bel-Air (but those are two far disparate stories). All that, and I have 4 kids to keep me on my toes. Needless to say, I have my hands full right now.

If you'd told me three years ago that I'd be writing an entire series of novels based on the concept of warlocks, elves, dwarves, and all manner of fantasy beings existing in the historical background of the Wild West, I might have considered it possible, though not probable. I was deep into drafting hard Science Fiction at that time, and viewed Fantasy as something best left to the long, plodding epics that seemed to dominate the genre in the early 21st century. Though, as it turns out, there is room for more condensed tales in the genre, so long as they're original in some way... and entertaining!

Magic in the Wild West? You don't get more entertaining or original than that! That's my story, and I'm sticking to it.

As I'm writing this, the second book in the series is in the late production stages, and will be hitting the shelves in mere weeks. It will continue the amazing adventures of a dwarven gunslinger, a warlock sheriff, and a feisty elvish widow in the mythical landscape of Nye County, Nevada in the 1880's.

Speaking of the setting, when I first wrote the short story, "A Dwarf at high Noon," I hadn't planned on a firm setting. It was still an abstract idea, and the original short was just something I threw together one afternoon on a whim. The idea of *where* Selwood, Nevada was hadn't crossed my mind.

When it came time to write a full-length feature, the location needed to be firmly established. While I could have gone with a totally historical background, and set Selwood in amidst pre-existing towns and cities, I decided in the grand tradition of Fantasy to draft my own "map" of the area; to do some "world building." So, I re-envisioned the landscape, making this alternate Nye County a far more developed area than it ever was in our reality. This was the only major historical change I made to the western landscape, and it isn't much different than what some authors of traditional Westerns have done in the past.

With this special Second Edition release, I've sought to maintain the integrity of the original. The main story remains as it first appeared in the Hall Brothers Entertainment release, with some minor formatting changes and one major extra. Preceding the main story you'll have the chance to read the original short story, "A Dwarf at High Noon." Prior to this release, that story has only ever been available in HBE's "Villainy" anthology.

Within these pages, we have the genesis of my Fantasy Western Saga. Enjoy a momentary diversion from reality, as you step back in time to the West the way it wasn't.

-Martin T. Ingham
December 13, 2012

TABLE OF CONTENTS

BONUS CONTENT

WEST OF THE WARLOCK

Prologue:
A Dwarf at High Noon

It was raining in Selwood, a rare drizzle for the arid Nevada town. It was somehow fitting, Ron thought, as his horse trotted down Main Street beneath his stout form. The inclement weather mimicked his mood, and steadied his resolve. Such things he had on his mind, and none of them worthy of sunlight.

The foul climate didn't bother him, and it was a familiar scene from his childhood back east. *Such a strange place, this western expanse.* He wondered what his grandfather would have thought, had he known about this land called America. It was all a far cry from the dwarven subcities of Europe and Asia Minor, where his people had been forced to live underground for centuries. Here, in this brave new world, a dwarf could show his face up above, without fear of persecution—for the most part.

Despite the rain, there were people out and about. Businessmen, ranchers, craftsmen, and miners walked proudly, each distinct in their individual attire. A few ladies roamed the streets with stylish umbrellas, and Ron made sure to give them a wink in passing. They didn't seem to mind.

Most of the buildings were the same gray color, the shade of weathered wood, but one structure stood out, painted a distinct white. It was there that Ron was headed, the Lucca Saloon, which would determine his fate.

After hitching his horse to the rail outside, Ron sauntered inside the saloon, his chaps scuffing with each step. The swinging doors were no taller than his chest as he pushed through them and found the dingy atmosphere of the establishment. The kerosene lamps provided some illumination on a gloomy day, but not all of them were burning. The handful of midday patrons didn't warrant a waste of fuel.

With an undignified jolt, Ron threw himself onto a barstool near the taps. From the higher perch, he could look the bartender in the eye, and gauge his responses as only a dwarf could.

"Don't see many of your kind in here," the elf said with a snide inflection. He didn't match the profile of your average barkeep, looking more like a wealthy aristocrat with his silk shirt and neatly-styled hair. Most elves were like that; respectable to a fault.

"I'm looking for someone," Ron grumbled. "Fellow by the name of Vincent Lafayette. Maybe you've heard of him?"

The elf replied with a smile. "Oh, yes, I know Vint."

"Can you tell me where to find him?" Ron asked.

"Yes," the elf answered, but said no more.

"Well, tell me," Ron requested.

"No."

"What?"

"You asked if I could tell you, not if I would," the elf replied arrogantly.

"You dirty little sneak," Ron snapped, shoving a finger under the elf's nose. "If you know what's good for ya, you'll start talking."

The elf blinked nervously, as if he hadn't expected the outburst, and slid his left hand over an orb sitting beside the taps. A carefully practiced stroke of the glass ball produced a distinct glow, signaling the successful activation of the mystical device.

A bright flash of light appeared behind Ron, and he turned to see a new figure had arrived. The leather-clad individual with a long trench coat and badge pinned to his chest was easily identifiable.

"Sheriff Doliber," the elf greeted him.

"Solen," the sheriff replied, leaning an arm against the counter. "What's the matter?"

"This leprechaun spoke to me in a most threatening manner," Solen replied.

"Hey!" Ron exclaimed.

"See what I mean?" Solen added.

"Yeah, I see," Doliber replied.   "You've been poking a bear, again."

"I beg your pardon?"

"You call the dwarf a Mick and wonder why he gets irate. Really, Solen, one of these days..."

The elf replied with a blank expression.

Doliber snapped his fingers, and the next thing Ron knew he was falling over, as the stool vanished from beneath him. Getting back on his feet, he realized it wasn't just the stool that was gone, but the entire saloon. He'd been teleported to the sheriff's office.

"Now we can talk," Doliber said, walking over to his desk.

"A mystic lawman?" Ron remarked as he found a chair.

"Journeyman Warlock, Delta Grade, at your service," Doliber replied as he lowered himself into a leather chair. "Cigar?" he asked, as he removed a pair of slender sticks from a box on his desk.

Ron declined, having never acquired a taste for tobacco.

"Yes, wizardry skills certainly help in this line of work," Doliber remarked as a mystic flame appeared in mid-air, lighting his cigar. "I've given most of the local businesses in this county a call-orb, so I can visit at a moment's notice. Now, what's your business here, dwarf?"

Ron sat in the creaky wooden chair in front of the desk as he replied. "Like I told the elf, I'm looking for Vincent Lafayette."

Doliber blew out a cloud of smoke and frowned beneath his mustache. "What for?"

"It's a personal matter," Ron said, reluctant to admit his reasons to the sheriff.

"Oh, I'm sure," Doliber said with a knowing nuance. "It's got to be personal when you want to kill a man."

"Who said anything about killing?"

"Empathy's another skill that comes in handy in my line of work. I can sense your hatred. You're looking for blood."

"You would, too, if Lafayette had killed your brother," Ron answered through his teeth.

"And you would be?"

"Boron Grimes."

"You're Darrell's brother?" Doliber asked with a scrutinizing stare. "You look similar, but that beard kinda hides it."

"You knew him?"

"Only in passing. He was an honest prospector, and while I wouldn't be surprised if Lafayette killed him, there's no proof."

"I've got all the proof I need, in here," Ron said, tapping the side of his head.

"Mind explaining?"

"Dwarf siblings share a psychic bond in some cases; nothing major, but when my brother died he sent his final thoughts through the ether, and I picked them up. I got a name and a face, and a whole load of pain along with it."

"What did you see?"

"Vincent Lafayette shot my brother in the back, twice, then rolled him over and put one between the eyes. I don't know why, but I intend to get an answer."

"That's going to be tough," Doliber said.

"Why? You intend to stop me, sheriff?" Ron asked.

"Actually, I'd like to help you. Lafayette's bad news. He's notorious for killing rivals in duels, and I'm sure he's left a few unmarked graves in the wild. If you want to challenge him, I won't stop you, but if you want to succeed you'll need my help."

"Why?"

"There's a reason he's such a lucky duelist, and it's more than just his shooting skills. Also, you should know he's half elf."

Ron groaned at the confirmation. He'd thought as much from the image in his brother's memory, but he'd been hoping it was just cosmetic. Going up against an elf complicated things, in so many ways.

"I guess that explains the bartender's attitude," Ron mentioned.

"Yes, they're a fiercely loyal race, and they have no qualms about bending the rules or breaking the law when it comes to protecting their own, even a half-breed like Lafayette. His outlaw gang—all of them elves—will support him to the bitter end. That's a dangerous thing, but with my help you could change all that, *Deputy* Grimes."

Doliber opened a desk drawer and retrieved a bright, silver badge from within. With a flick of his wrist, he tossed it at Ron, smacking the dwarf squarely in the chest. Instead of simply bounding off, the metal pinned itself to Ron's chest; all thanks to a little magic.

"I'm not interested in being one of your lackeys," Ron complained.

"You'd better be, if you intend to go against Lafayette. Shut up and listen to my plan, and maybe we'll stand a chance of delivering that justice you're after."

* * *

It was late afternoon on Friday before Vincent Lafayette rode into Selwood with his elvish gang. The rain was long gone, and dry air once more dominated the landscape, permitting a cloud of dust to drift in the wake of their Sand Mares. Looking more dragon than horse, the ghastly steeds thundered down Main Street, their clawed feet churning up bits of dirt with each step. They were far from graceful, but their speed was unmatched by any mammalian equine.

The saloon was fairly empty as the tall man with black stubble swaggered through the door, with enough sweat and stink on him to scare a starving vulture. The quiet room echoed his footsteps as he made his way to the bar and slid onto the stool in front of the taps.

"How's business, Solen?" Lafayette asked, reaching over to slap the bartender on the shoulder.

"Slow, Vint," Solen replied, pulling a bottle of aged whiskey out from under the counter. "Damned temperance movement's got too many folks abstaining. Curse those blasted Mormons!"

"Guess that leaves more for us, right, boys?" Lafayette cheered to his gang, who all grinned with mouths of stained and crooked teeth. These lawless elves hardly resembled their old-world brethren, but the ears gave them away.

Solen poured a double shot of fine Kentucky bourbon for Lafayette, then began filling mugs of ale for the others. He'd serviced these men for years, and knew their individual tastes.

"So, what's new?" Lafayette asked after downing his first double. "Anything interesting going on?"

"There was one thing," Solen remarked. "A dwarf stopped here looking for you the other day."

"Oh, really?" Lafayette asked, sounding less than surprised. "Bet we could guess what he was after."

"Hard time guessin' whose kin it'ud be, seein' how we's kilt so many of them midgies," one of his snaggle-toothed comrades opined.

"So, what happened to him?" Lafayette asked the bartender.

"He was rude, so I had the sheriff haul him away," Solen said, pouring Lafayette another shot.

"Sorry I missed it," Lafayette replied. "Haven't had a good runt toss in months. You'd think they were avoiding me, or something."

The gang of elves laughed on cue.

"Speaking of avoidance," Solen mentioned, "your tab is getting heavy. With business the way it is, I hope you could make a partial payment... sometime."

Lafayette grinned and slapped the bartender on the shoulder again. "No worries, Solen. I'll have enough to square us up before I leave town."

"Are you sure? It's a very heavy tab."

"Oh, you'd be surprised," Lafayette said. "The claim we *acquired* from that Grimy midge a few months back, it's a literal gold mine. Soon as I visit the assayer's office, we'll be richer than a twenty dollar whore."

Solen raised his brows at the analogy, appreciating the full meaning. His ladies were only two dollars a visit, and they brought in a tidy sum for themselves and the house. He could only dream of the wealth one might acquire at ten times their current hourly rates.

"Speaking of which, is Tina available?" Lafayette asked.

"Indeed," Solen replied. "Like I said, business is slow... but I guess things'll be picking up."

* * *

Evening brought a modest crowd to the Lucca Saloon, as the working residents of Selwood came to eat, drink, and play games. Despite Solen's claims of poor business, things looked pretty hopping to Ron Grimes, as he walked in for the second time.

Every seat was filled, and the packed house concealed his movements as he walked to a corner table where quiet men played poker. Sheriff Doliber's mystic intel told him this was where he would find Lafayette.

"I'd shoot you in the back, but I don't do things your way," Ron said as he stood behind his quarry.

Lafayette tilted his head back, seeking the owner of the voice. "Oh, look, a midge," he said, turning around to face the man who stood neck high to the saloon chairs.

"You killed my brother," Ron said, trying to keep cool. Anger raged through him, enough to make him want a quick resolution, but he knew he had to do this a certain way.

"I've killed so many of you runts over the years," Lafayette bragged. "Which one was your brother?"

"Darrell Grimes."

"Sorry, I don't usually get their names."

"Two months ago, he was the prospector you shot."

"Oh, him. Yes, now I see the family resemblance. Though, all you midges look pretty much the same, don't you?"

"You killed him just for being a dwarf?" Ron asked, seeking an explanation.

"He was sitting on my claim, so me and the boys evicted him. But between you and me, I'd have killed him just for the fun of it."

"Your claim, indeed," Ron said dubiously. "You murdered him for his land, didn't you?"

"Now that's a damn lie," Lafayette growled. "You better watch yourself, midge." Seeking to end their conversation, he turned back to the card table.

"You're the liar here, Lafayette!" Ron shouted. "You killed my brother and stole his claim. I dare you to prove otherwise."

Lafayette jumped to his feet, knocking over his chair which nearly hit Ron. "You spit on my good name, you rot! You asked for it. Draw!" He set a hand on the Colt Peacemaker hanging from his hip.

"Hey!" a shout came from the bar. Solen rushed over, pushing past the apprehensive crowd. "You want to kill the midge, do it outside."

"Fine by me," Lafayette said.

One of Lafayette's henchmen tugged at his sleeve. "Say, boss, it's mighty dark out there."

Lafayette growled in frustration. "Alright, we'll settle it tomorrow, bright and early, assuming you've got the manhood!"

"At noon," Ron countered.

"Why wait?" Lafayette asked.

"I want to see you sweat," Ron said, walking backwards. He kept his face on Lafayette as he made his way out, fearing the bandit's bloodlust may outweigh his patience.

Once outside, Ron mounted his horse and rode down the street to the sheriff's office, where Doliber awaited.

"Everything's set," Ron said as he entered.

"I know," Doliber replied, having observed everything remotely on a magic mirror. He pointed a thumb at the sheet behind him, which displayed a real-time view of the saloon's interior.

"Nice trick," Ron said. "Are we ready?"

"I will be. Just make sure you don't miss tomorrow."

* * *

Dueling was currently legal in Nevada, but it was rare to have anything scheduled. Fights were usually spur of the moment, and concluded within minutes. In other circumstances, a good night's rest often sobered up rivals, allowing for a more peaceful resolution to disputes. This was not the case today, however, for both Vincent Lafayette and Boron Grimes were eager to see the other bleed.

The sun was high, and Ron looked at his large, bronze pocket watch, confirming the approaching hour. Two minutes shy of noon, and here he stood in the center of Main Street. A few riders trotted by, but most people were lined up on either side of the road, waiting to see the contest.

Lafayette sauntered out of the Lucca saloon and took his position, grinning all the while.

As the church bell rang noon, both men reached for their revolvers.

Ron yanked his old Remington out of its holster, cocked the hammer with the palm of his left hand and squeezed the trigger with his right forefinger, all in one swift motion. The thunderous crack of the shot filled the air, and a cloud of white smoke drifted out of the pistol's muzzle.

Lafayette didn't have a chance to fire before Ron's bullet sank into his flesh. Grabbing his chest in agony, he stumbled forward and fell over, planting his face in the parched earth. None of his gang came to his aid, but a lone doctor hurried over, took a look, and shook his head. With the medical opinion given, others from the crowd moved in to stare at the dying man and make their own assessments.

Ron walked over to his fallen opponent, hoping to confirm his accuracy. After pushing through the few dozen gawkers, he knelt down beside Lafayette and examined the half-elf's bloody shirt. It was hard to see where the bullet had entered, though the shot had obviously been on target.

"How'd you do that?" Lafayette uttered with his dying breath.

"Fair and square, that's how," Ron replied. He doubted the man was alive enough to hear him, but it felt good to say it. He had won. His brother was avenged, and this murderer would never kill again.

With the challenge over, Ron walked back to the sheriff's office, to see how Doliber had fared. He found the law man sitting behind his desk, smoking a cigar, grinning profusely as shouts of protest echoed out of the cells in the back room.

"Sounds like we have company," Ron mentioned as he sat down.

"If we didn't, you'd be dead," Doliber replied. "As I suspected, Lafayette's been rigging his duels, having his gang cast spells to deflect his opponents' bullets. I caught them dead to rights. Fixing duels like that makes it murder. They'll hang for it."

"Clearly, those amateurs were no match for a Warlock sheriff," Ron complimented.

"And their leader was no match for a real gunslinger," Doliber reciprocated.

"Lafayette was pretty lethargic out there," Ron mentioned. "Of course, knowing he could actually get shot might have sped him up a bit."

"I guess we'll never know," Doliber said as he snuffed out his cigar in a brass ashtray. "So, what are your plans now?"

"I figure I'll ride out to my brother's claim, see if I can find his body. After that, I might go prospecting."

"You do that, but keep yourself handy," Doliber said, putting his feet up on his desk. He leaned back and grinned at the dwarf. "You're still a deputy, remember?"

"Hey, that's not fair," Ron protested. "I never signed up for anything like that."

"You're the one who wanted justice. Accept the consequences," Doliber dug a silver dollar out of his shirt pocket and tossed it to Ron. "Here's your first paycheck. I'll call when I need you again."

"You do that," Ron said as he turned to leave.

Episode One:
The Stagecoach Heist

The dust of the hills rolled up in great plumes behind the stagecoach, as it thundered down the well-traveled road. The blued steel plates glistened in the late-afternoon sun, an armored behemoth among parched sagebrush. It was the pride of the fleet, owned and operated by Ferguson and Finney Limited. The mining consortium had a dozen coaches that made trips between Sacramento and Selwood, but this one was special, for transporting the most valuable cargoes.

The beasts hauling the coach were not horses, but sand mares. The cold-blooded reptilians looked more akin to dragons than equines, with scales and thorny protrusions covering them from head to tail. Six of the bulky creatures were attached to the yokes, and even with the heavy load they could outrun the fastest racehorse. The wild version native to the southern Rockies and Sierra Nevadas could turn you into a tasty snack with ease, though the domesticated variety were gentle enough, and could gallop in a smooth fashion.

Atop the armored coach sat a round cylinder of menacing armaments; the famed Gatling gun, the greatest machine gun of the day. With a few turns of the crank, it could fend off a pack of angry Indians, or slaughter the most ruthless elven bandits. Additional backup lurked inside the coach, as a pair of well-armed men waited with rifles and pistols, prepared to defend the cargo with their lives.

None could stand against the combined strength of these

defenses which sought to safeguard this special transport, or so the stockholders hoped.

The man smiled. He's seen it all before. Similar weapons had done no good last week for a band of disagreeable elves. The pointies really thought that a few hunks of metal and a few guns could stand up to his might, but he'd shown them. The rowdy claim-jumpers who'd wanted to hoard a mother load of antimony had tasted his wrath, and not one had lived to tell of it.

That had merely been a warm up. Today, the warlock in black would prove his true mettle.

Rubbing at his chin, the warlock felt the start of stubble growing there, and his thoughts momentarily shifted to his personal hygiene. He was never one for beards, and he'd be damned if he'd grow one like the old stuffed shirts at the academy. How careless he was being, forgetting to shave over the excitement of a heist. That could not be tolerated.

With a thought and a rolling of his eyes, the man activated the magic at his command, and a ripple of red rolled down his face, removing the tiny stubble growing on his cheeks and chin. The end result was a perfect shave, smoother than the best barber could provide. He stroked himself appreciatively, and decided he was ready.

Stretching out his arm, the man formulated a magic spell in his head, and directed it toward the charging sand mares. A scarcely visible streak of light flashed through the air and shot into each of the animals, disrupting their central nervous systems. Paralyzed, they stopped dead in their tracks, and began to tumble from their remaining inertia.

Under ordinary circumstances, a stagecoach would flip over, or even end-for-end after such an abrupt stop, but the added weight of the armor plates prevented the thing from toppling. Its back wheels lurched up in the air a couple of feet, then came back down with a great crash, bringing everything to a halt.

With the coach motionless, it would be such a simple task for any parlor magician to teleport the wealth inside, or so the man in black believed until he tried. Clearly, the brains behind this armored wagon's design had anticipated the possibility of mystic assault, and laced the exterior with a neutralizing ward. Your typical warlock or elvish bandit would find it impossible to extract anything from within the vehicle, though there was nothing typical about this darkly clothed gentleman. If he wished, he could defeat the magic wards, and take what he desired with a thought, though encountering resistance made him bold, and eager to face his foes in person.

"Time to say hello," he mused to himself, pulling a revolver out from under his coat. He clambered down the hill, stirring up a visible cloud of dust in the process. As he reached the road in front of the crippled coach, his eyes quickly locked onto the Gatling gun being trained upon him. Slowing down, he smiled in amusement at the shiny new weapon that sought to stand in his way.

The first shots resounded, sending .45 caliber bullets flying out past the speed of sound, seeking to shred the man's flesh, but they never got the chance. As the lead projectiles neared, the man froze each of them in place with a single wave of his hand. More and more piled into the air, but none could penetrate the thickness of the air molecules in front of this mystic bandit.

In the mounting seconds of gunfire, the man's attention drifted for a nanosecond to the fabric of reality around him. He perceived the bullets beyond their outward appearance, saw the subatomic bonds holding the atoms together, and marveled at the simplicity of it all. But it wasn't a single atom that held his attention, but millions of millions, all at once, reflected within his mind's eye. So much data that so few men could comprehend, yet he could see it all!

In the blink of an eye, his attention returned to the matter at hand, and the gray patch of bullets floating in front of him. The rattle of the Gatling gun had stopped, but three hundred bullets remained in close proximity to one another, hovering in mid-air, waiting for orders. Utilizing the stored inertia within the projectiles, the man redirected them, sending the barrage back at their source. The hunks of lead pelted the sides of the stagecoach. Their soft material did little to harm the hefty steel plates, but made a raucous noise, enough to frighten those who lurked inside the vehicle.

The man in black stretched his consciousness to see those who stood against him. He sensed their fear, and savored it, much as a wine taster samples a fine vintage. So raw and pure, yet simple in texture. How he longed for that sort of emotion, a basic feeling undiluted by extraneous knowledge beyond human existence. The sort of feeling he'd once shared not so long ago.

"They don't know how lucky they are," he thought, stepping up to the armored coach. "Ignorance is such bliss."

The metal was smooth as he slid a hand against a side plate. Closing his eyes, he sensed all the days and weeks that had transpired to craft this metal into its current form. He saw the miners extracting the raw ore, watched blacksmiths melt it in the crucible and shape it into sheets. He saw the machinists mill the sheets to the proper dimensions and rivet them into place. So much information from a simple touch. Sometimes, his power amazed even him.

Knowing the object so intimately had its advantages, for as he peered into its essence, he was able to manipulate the subatomic structure and reshape it at will. Setting his fingers at the edge of one plate, the metal gave way, allowing him a firm grip. With a yank of his arms, the inch of solid steel peeled and crumpled like a piece of thin foil, exposing the wooden framework of the coach and the men lurking inside.

There were two of them, and the warlock already knew all about them from his previous telepathic scans. Sampson Blascoe and Blaine McGruber, a couple of rough and tough Indian fighters who'd done a lot of slaughtering for the Union Army over the last decade. Now they were eking out a living in this cushy assignment, working security for Ferguson and Finney. They were about to meet their doom.

Blascoe was front and center, ready to do his job to the bitter end. He'd faced his fair share of native Shamans and Medicine Men and figured that experience could save his sorry backside today. Squeezing the trigger on his revolver and fanning the hammer with the heel of his hand, he sent six slugs in quick succession into his adversary's chest, confident that they'd do the job. The projectiles were no ordinary bullets. They'd been treated with a fine coating of Basilisk blood, giving them a strong resistance to mystic energy other than their own.

The bullets stung like fire as they punched through the warlock's flesh. The typical forcefield he'd summoned did nothing to halt their progress. He hadn't anticipated this turn of events, and marveled at the unexpected turnaround. It had been so long since anything had surprised him, it made for a neat change of pace.

Healing injuries was elementary, and for a fleeting moment the warlock felt certain it would be easy, but the same energy that had negated his protective magic was still at work, only on a far more invasive level. He felt the flesh around the holes hardening, as the trace of Basilisk blood worked its sinister task. If left unchecked, his body would be solid stone in a matter of minutes.

"Heh, gotcha!" Blascoe shouted in joy.

The warlock grimaced as the wounds continued to sting with icy pain, and he fought for the proper counteragent to repel the petrification. His mastery of magic was virtually unmatched. How could he be felled by this simpleton and a few drops of a lizard's blood?

Then, the answer came.

Peering into the subatomic yet again, the warlock saw the energies at work, saw them as colorful waves ripping and tearing at molecules within his body. He saw his own mystical energies intermingled there, unable to defeat the petrifying spell of the Basilisk. Drawn into this unique trance, the solution was delivered to him; a way to reshape his own spell and cancel the magic attacking his cells.

With the blink of an eye, the pain went away. The transmutation ceased, allowing the warlock to heal his injuries with ease. As the holes in his stomach disappeared, the smile on Blascoe's face vanished with them.

"Tough break, Sammy," the warlock said, regaining his own smirk. Ah, what a satisfying turnaround!

Blascoe was fighting to eject the spent cases from his revolver as quickly as possible. One by one, the ejector rod pushed the empty brass from the cylinder, but it was futile. His time had run out.

The warlock still had a revolver in his left hand. He'd been gripping it this whole time, waiting for the chance to use it. The simple mechanical device with its neatly polished parts and ornately-carved ivory grips was a marvel of modern machinery, and with this fine weapon the warlock put down his foe in a most material manner. Three shots were placed in slow succession, enough to grant him added satisfaction from the kill. Blascoe crumpled to the ground in a lifeless heap, leaving only one man standing between this warlock and the gold.

Blaine McGruber saw the futility in resistance, and threw up his hands. In response, the warlock put a bullet in his gut, unwilling to accept the man's obvious surrender.

Stepping into the armored coach, the warlock kept his pistol aimed at Blaine, who struggled against the pain. "Take it," the wounded guard said, staggering away from the locked safe.

"Oh, I intend to," the warlock said, sticking his pistol in McGruber's face, eager to finish the job. "I'm still going to kill you."

"But... why?" McGruber asked in agony, staring down the barrel pointed at his forehead.

"Because I can," the warlock said, cocking the hammer, "and because I must."

The shot rang out, sending McGruber to his maker, and leaving the warlock with his spoils.

The safe wasn't that large, a cubical block about two feet square, though there was only so much a team of beasts could haul. The warlock wasted no time dismantling the locks, and took special care to detect any mysticism afoot. As expected, there was a ward cast on the safe, which would have paralyzed any common lock-picker, but not a true master of magic. The ward was dispelled and the door creaked open to reveal the contents within.

Several dozen bags of gold dust sat inside the safe, close to a thousand pounds of precious metal. The small fortune was a pleasing sight, though it was only one of the warlock's objectives. Removing the bags with haste, he made his way to the bottom of the safe, which appeared to be nothing out of the ordinary at first glance. However, upon close inspection, faint lines could be seen in the metal plate near the back: a hidden compartment!

With careful attention, the warlock formulated the proper spell to pry up the plate without disturbing the contents underneath it. There, as the metal gave way, he saw what he was looking for, a slender pewter box scarcely smaller than the hole it was sitting in. He levitated it out of its hiding place and into his waiting hands, grinning profusely.

The contents of this little box could be the key to all his hopes and dreams. How funny, he wasn't even sure what it was. He'd killed these men and robbed this stage coach, all for something he'd never seen. How he longed to inspect the merchandise, but he'd been instructed to keep the box shut, and deliver the contents undisturbed. Yet, considering the effort he'd expended and all the blood on his hands, he had to find out what this box held. What could be so powerful that it would warrant such wanton destruction in its retrieval?

His curiosity was too much to bear, and he found himself reaching a finger into the slender groove, eager to peek inside.

* * *

The last clump of dirt fell from Ron Grimes' shovel, as he laid his brother to rest. This was the least he could do for his kin, even though the smell had been unbearable. The body had been left in a dark cave for the better part of three months before Ron had found it. Only the arid environment had preserved it enough for identification.

"I got 'em, Darrell," Ron said to his brother's spirit. "I shot your killer fair and square." He tossed his shovel aside and placed the wide-brimmed cowboy hat over his heart. Closing his eyes, he said a little prayer in his head, wishing he could remember a divine scripture. He'd never been heavy on religion, despite his parents' insistence. Too old world, he'd always said.

The sun was hot in the Nevada desert, so Ron didn't leave his hat off for long. His thinning hair did little to protect his scalp from the elements. The signs of age were catching up with him, and he had little to show for the passing years. He'd found no fortune, owned little more than the clothes on his back, and what family he had left was sitting in the ground under his feet.

This was a sad state for a dwarf approaching middle-age.

Leaving his brother's grave, Ron climbed atop his horse and moved on, across the arid wastes. There was really no reason for him to hang around. This worthless hunk of land that had been his brother's claim didn't hold his interest. If there was gold here, he didn't see it, and mining had never been his forte.

He was twenty miles from Selwood, that populated crossroads in the center of this arid expanse. His horse was pointed in that direction, but did he really want to go back? His business there was done; his brother's murder avenged. The only reason he'd want to stick around would be to please the local sheriff, who sought to keep Ron as an indentured deputy.

A little voice in the back of Ron's mind told him to get out, make for the county line, and never look back. Hell, forget the county, get out of the entire state! There was nothing he wanted in Nevada, and there were plenty of other places out west where a dwarf could make his mark, and get a little peace. Maybe find a spread in Oregon or Idaho, where the hunting was good and there was plenty of water. Wherever he ended up, it would be better than here.

His mind was made. Spurring his horse with his heels and snapping the reins, Ron was off, heading northwest. It would be a long ride, but there were other towns and watering holes in his path... or, at least, there would have been if he'd been kept on course.

Suddenly, a flash of darkness appeared over Ron's eyes, and in the blink of an eye he found himself falling. The horse was gone from beneath him, along with the dusty hills. Wooden floorboards were coming up fast, and he tucked himself into a ball and rolled as he landed to avoid serious injury. After coming to a stop and jumping to his feet, he looked around the familiar room, and realized exactly what had happened.

"Blast you, Doliber!" Ron shouted as he turned toward the desk where the local sheriff was sitting.

"Sorry for the abrupt teleport, but I couldn't have you running off on me," Sheriff Doliber replied, picking a cigar out of the box on his desk. With a snap of his fingers, a mystic spark ignited the tip, and the embers glowed as he inhaled.

"You've been spying on me," Ron said with certainty. He'd feared as much, knowing the sheriff's mystic talents.

Doliber tapped the side of his right temple. "Empathic link, remember? I can sense what you're feeling, and your flight instincts blared out loud and clear a few minutes ago. You were trying to split."

"Damn it, Doliber, I told you I don't want anything more to do with you. Our business is finished."

"We're finished when I say we are," Doliber replied, tapping his cigar against his ornate, brass ashtray. There wasn't much ash in the receptacle, showing he had recently cleaned it.

"Why won't you just let me go?" Ron asked, feeling as caged as any prisoner.

"Because I need you," Doliber admitted. "You've seen the kind of characters who operate around here. I can't deal with them alone."

"I'm sure you can manage, considering all that warlock training of yours."

"Even I have my limits. Reliable help's hard to come by, and you're one of the sharpest gunslingers I've ever seen. Wouldn't you like to put those talents to good use?"

"No," Ron said defiantly.

Doliber sighed. "Why are you so resistant? You're not a wicked man, and you certainly aren't a coward. What's got you running scared?"

"That's my business," Ron said, knowing the sheriff was looking to guilt him. It wasn't going to work. He'd done his duty, and done enough killing for one lifetime. He wasn't about to get drafted again.

"All right, look, things are pretty calm right now, so why don't you take a load off, settle in for a few days. Think things over, and if you really can't bring yourself to do the right thing, I'll let you go."

"Waiting around a few days isn't going to change my mind," Ron replied. He'd already spent a week in the hills, thinking about the sheriff's offer, and he'd made his decision.

"Even so, it won't hurt you to get some rest before you trudge off to wherever it is you're going. The Bormans have a boarding house on the edge of town. I'll pay for your room."

"I don't need your charity," Ron grumbled.

"Consider it a signing bonus if you accept the job, or severance pay if you don't. Either way, the room is paid for."

"Thanks," Ron said, turning to leave. He'd been in Nevada

almost a month already, so what was another few days? A free room was nothing to balk at, in any case. As he reached the door, another concern crossed his mind. "Say, what about my horse?"

"He's right outside," Doliber assured him. "I'll book him a stall at Kinney's livery stable while you check out the boarding house."

"You do that," Ron said, heading out the door.

Outside, the midday sun was beating down on the dusty streets of Selwood. The town was pretty busy, serving as a central hub of travel in southern Nevada. Prospectors, gamblers, gunfighters, and freeholders could all be found browsing the shops and drinking at the saloon. The town itself didn't have that many full-time residents, but the countryside poured in for the amenities.

Ron found the Bormans' boarding house easily enough, and checked in. The elderly lady tending the place gave him a quick tour of his room, a ten by twelve box with a bed and a weathered washtub that a full-sized human would be cramped in. Though, a dwarf could find the half-barrel basin relaxing, assuming the thing didn't give him a splinter. He had two weeks of dust and sweat stuck to his skin, so a bath was most desired, and his first order of business.

It would take at least an hour for Mrs. Borman to heat enough water for the tub, but Ron was used to roughing it, so he took it cold. Using a complimentary bar of soap, he scrubbed himself down until the water was black. He regretted that he only had the one set of clothes, as he put the filthy garments on his clean skin. Perhaps that could be remedied.

The sheriff's offer was starting to interest him, even if he didn't want to admit it. He could certainly use the money, no doubt about it, though the thought of fighting for a living no longer appealed to him. He had enough blood on his hands already. Many jobs in his youth had been violent, whether it was fighting Rebs in the Civil War, or wild Indians in the Dakotas, or drunken cattle rustlers in Oklahoma; he'd seen more than his fair share of combat. He was tired of killing for a living.

But he was so good at it.

With the clothes on his back, he cycled the cylinder of his Remington revolver. The old cap-and-ball design was pretty antiquated in this era of cartridges, but it had seen him through many scrapes.   It wasn't so much the tool, as the craftsman wielding it that mattered.

Strapping the six-shooter to his hip, Ron's hand brushed against his right pocket, and felt the hunk of metal protruding from within. He reached in and dug out the silver badge Doliber had pinned on him a while back, the shiny star of authority. The allure of power was not lost on him, though the duty and responsibility was a heavy counterweight.

Part of him wanted to fling the badge out a window, but the little voice in the back of his mind forced him to pocket the thing again.

"A few days, he says," Ron mumbled to himself. "Great."

Walking down Main Street, Ron decided to check on his horse. He knew where the livery stable was, so he took a quick detour and made sure the sheriff had stuck to his word. Sure enough, Ron found his trusted companion wedged in a stall, waiting patiently to revisit the trail. It set his mind at ease, as he continued his journey to the Lucca Saloon.

Reaching the town's primary drinking establishment, Ron pushed open the swinging doors and walked over to the counter, then heaved himself up onto a waiting stool. His approach had been observed by the prim and proper elf waiting by the taps. Ron remembered the bartender from his last visit to Selwood, and knew he was stirring up trouble by coming here.

"Well, if it isn't the Leprechaun again," Solen remarked arrogantly, brushing a hand over his neatly-combed blond hair.

"I ain't no Irishman, you pointy-eared dandy," Ron grumbled. "Now, gimme a whiskey."

"I'm sorry, but we don't serve *your* kind in here," Solen replied with a smile.

"My kind?" Ron smiled back and dug the deputy badge out of his pocket. "What, you mean law men?" The badge rattled on the hardwood counter in front of Solen.

Solen sighed and rolled his eyes.

"Whiskey!" Ron growled.

"Are you on duty?" Solen asked.

"Does that matter?"

"I couldn't in good conscience serve you while you're on-duty."

"Fine, then I'm off duty," Ron answered, putting the badge away.

"Well, then I'm afraid we don't serve your kind in here," Solen replied.

The intentional slight burned on Ron's nerves, as his emotional state was already pretty raw from recent events. Grabbing the cocky elf by his broad lapels, he growled back, "Look here, pointy, I'm not playing your twisted little games. I ain't had a drink in six months, and I'm sure as hell gonna get that whiskey, one way or another. Now, you can either get paid for it, or I'll confiscate it in the name of the law. It's your choice."

"Who do you think you are?" Solen asked with a shrill voice. "This is America. I have rights!"

Ron grunted in amusement, and released his grip on the elf's jacket. "Yeah, even a pointy-eared bugger like you has 'em, and so do I. Now, sell me a damn drink."

Solen brushed his jacket, as if shaking off dirt. "Well, since you asked so nicely..." He turned and grabbed a brown bottle from the rack behind him, and proceeded to fill a shot glass with the tan liquid. "Two bits."

Ron dug into his pocket and found a few pieces of silver. Besides the silver dollar, he had a couple of twenty-cent pieces. He'd won the odd things at a Faro table in Kansas City a few months back, and for a while there he'd suspected a fraud. *Who'd ever heard of a twenty cent piece?* It had only been since hitting Nevada that he'd seen the things in regular use, though even here they weren't that popular.

The silver coins jingled against the hardwood counter. "How about two shots for forty?" Ron asked.

Solen grabbed the coins and smirked. "Don't press your luck, midge." He promptly produced three nickels in change, which Ron glared at before pocketing.

With the money paid, Ron finally got around to downing the shot. The rot-gut burned down his throat. It wasn't the nicest feeling, but after a few seconds, the warm buzz enveloped him, taking the edge off recent aches of his body and soul. One was enough, so he didn't regret the failed haggling. Still, he'd have felt bad if he hadn't at least tried to chisel the annoying bartender.

As the warmth of the drink took hold of him, he noticed a conspicuous figure clomping into the saloon.

Ron turned around slowly, and looked to see a woman stomping towards him. What he saw surprised him in many ways. The heavy leather attire looked wholly unsuited to a lady, though it couldn't hide her ample bosom, or the soft elegance of her face. Yes, there was something very alluring about this lady, even if she were a lousy elf.

"Are you Boron Grimes," the lady asked, staying a few steps away from the dwarf. She was shooting daggers with her eyes as he remained silent. "Well?"

There was no telling what this woman wanted, though Ron felt comfortable enough to finally answer. "I am, and you would be?"

"My name is Joella Lafayette-Talus. You shot my husband."

A surge of adrenaline pulsed through Ron's head, disrupting the pleasant buzz. His hand instinctually reached for the revolver tucked under his long jacket.

"Don't even try it," Joella snapped, pointing her own weapon in his face. She could have fired and ended his short existence then and there. The fact that she kept her finger off the trigger said that wasn't her immediate intent.

"Excuse me," Solen interrupted. "Do you two mind..."

"Stay out of this, barkeeper," Joella ordered with a shout. "You know Elvish Clan Law. Would you deny the rights of a widow?"

Solen rolled his eyes and stepped away from the counter, leaving Ron to face the angry woman on his own.

"What do you want with me?" Ron asked, staring down the barrel of her sleek Smith & Wesson.

"You killed my husband. What do you think I want?" Joella asked incredulously.

"Then shoot, and get it over with," Ron challenged, feeling his number was up. There was nothing he could do if she was intent on firing, so he turned back to his empty shot glass, showing it more interest than the pistol aimed at his head.

Joella narrowed her eyes in irritation. "Oh, I can't believe I'm doing this," she complained, grabbing at a small pouch tied to her belt. It took her a minute to get the knot untied with a single hand, but once the satin bag was released she dug two fingers inside and tossed a pinch of red dust in Ron's face.

The substance tingled like the whiskey, but it was far more powerful than simple drink. As Ron tried to speak, he found his throat paralyzed, and noticed the rest of his body going numb. What was this mad woman doing to him?

"You're going to pay, Grimes," Joella said as his eyes went dark and his limp body slid off the bar stool. "Just not how you might expect."

* * *

The call came in shortly after Ron Grimes left the sheriff's office; a mystic message from a summoning orb that Doliber had given to most every businessman in the county. If something came up, he could be contacted in a moment's notice, and respond instantly via a magic teleport. Having a warlock for a sheriff certainly had its advantages.

There was something different about this summons. The call wasn't from any of the populated towns, as usual, but from thirty miles northwest of Selwood, a patch of parched dust near the county line. That spelled trouble, for sure, so Doliber wasted no time with his reply. With a ceremonial flick of his wrist, he activated a mental command which sent him instantly to the source of the signal. A mild tingling sensation lingered as his body adjusted to its new surroundings.

Hills of dirt and rock, with a bit of scrub brush mixed in for character, greeted Doliber as the midday sun beat down overhead. Someone had called him to this?

"Hey, Jimmy," a voice grabbed Doliber's attention. He turned around to see a tall man in a beige trench coat smiling back. "Good of you to show up."

"Marshal Rodgers," Doliber greeted the man with suspicion. He'd met this federal law man on a few occasions, always in an official capacity. There was no love between the two of them, and their working relationship was tenuous, at best. The Marshal wouldn't have contacted the sheriff unless it was important.

The larger question remained. How had he summoned Doliber in the first place?

"Here, I think this is one of yours," Rodgers said, tossing a round, glass ball at Doliber.

"Where'd you get this?" Doliber asked, staring at the mystic orb. It was about the size of a billiard ball.

"On the other side of this ridge," Rodgers said, leading the way. The two men climbed the slight slope and peered over the other side at the mutilated stagecoach and the dead men within.

The familiar scent of death greeted Doliber as he stood before the wreckage. The foul odor of blood and entrails told that the kills were relatively fresh, no more than a few hours old. An ordinary man couldn't cross much territory in that time, but from the wrinkled steel plates and the dead mares without a scratch on them, it was obviously no ordinary man who'd done this.

"You can see why I called you," Marshal Rodgers said, rubbing his hands together nervously. "Looks like something in your league."

"Indeed," Doliber said, squeezing his eyes shut. The gesture was not a sign of irritation, but part of a trigger that activated a unique spell. As he opened his eyelids, a flash of blue light flickered over his vision and left his eyeballs aglow. The result gave him the ability to perceive the lingering traces of mystic energy lurking on the crime scene. Magnificent splotches of color coated all places that magic had touched, proving beyond a shadow of a doubt what Doliber had feared since first seeing the mangled coach.

This was not the work of a desert troll, or some elvish bandit. These were clearly human magic traces, which could mean only one thing. A fellow warlock was to blame; someone with real training, not just a parlor magician. Likely, a member of the Guild itself!

"So, whatcha got?" Rodgers asked, stroking his neatly trimmed mustache.

"A headache," Doliber replied.

EpisodeTwo:
Unintended Consequences

Ron woke up to shooting pain in his eyes. The sting was like shards of glass tearing at his corneas, and the glare he witnessed blinded him completely, like a hot desert sun. He began to tear up from the agony, even as he tried to move his body. Nothing. Something was restraining him so completely, he couldn't move from the neck down.

What had that elf strumpet done to him?

Blinking furiously, Ron sought to clear his sight, and found slight relief as the pain faded. Even as the blinding light disappeared, he remained unable to see, for there was darkness all around. The cold breeze on his face confirmed the presence of night, even as the twinkling stars became visible to his recovering eyes.

"I wouldn't thrash too much if I were you," Joella's voice called. "Essence of Red Moon can do a number on your muscles, even when you can't feel them."

"Release me now!" Ron ordered, jerking his neck in an attempt to gain some control over his torso. There was a tingling in his shoulders, which told him he was getting better. Impatience was spurred by apprehension, as he wondered what evil machinations this elvish widow had in store for him.

"You're not going anywhere," Joella answered. "Not until I get what I need."

Her enigmatic answer provided little comfort to Ron, as he ceased his struggling. There was no point fighting with unresponsive muscles. Though he couldn't fathom what Joella's true intentions were, it was clear she wasn't about to kill him; at least, not yet.

"Get some sleep," Joella advised. "We've got a long ride tomorrow."

"The sheriff's not going to take kindly to you kidnapping his deputy," Ron said, hoping to use his new status as persuasion.

"Oh, I wouldn't worry about Doliber too much," Joella said, sounding smug. "He's a bit preoccupied at the moment."

"What did you do to him?" Ron grumbled.

"Nothing," Joella answered. "Fate was simply kind enough to provide me with the perfect cover, so I took advantage of it. Now, save your strength for tomorrow. You'll need it."

Seeing no alternative, Ron lay back and wondered what fate had in store for him. It had never been terribly kind, though he was still alive, and that was something. Then again, maybe death was too good for him in the eyes of the creator?

Night passed quickly, with brief aches and pains preventing him from getting any real rest. By the time dawn came, he was grateful to be fully awake and have a look at his current surroundings.

Things weren't as desolate as he'd last recalled. The green bushes and pine trees told him he was a long way from Selwood, likely out of Nevada altogether. How long had he been unconscious? It would have taken days to ride this far—more likely Joella had used some form of teleportation magic to expedite their journey.

Well, it looked like he'd gotten his wish. He was beyond Doliber's control. Too bad he'd merely traded one master for another.

"Where are we?" Ron asked as Joella led him to the horse. Despite the resemblance, it wasn't his own, as was evident by the Elvish brand on the right hip and the lack of his custom double stirrup.

"California," Joella said, grabbing him by the britches and tossing him into his saddle. She did it with little effort, proving the strength of her muscles.

"Yeah, that's real helpful," Ron mentioned as he tried to get into a comfortable position. It was hard with his hands tied. "Exactly where in California are we going?"

"It's not far now," Joella said, remaining vague. "If we ride steady, we should be there before nightfall."

The foliage grew thicker as they traveled, turning into a full blown forest after a few hours. It slowed them down considerably, as the trails became less defined, though Joella seemed to know where she was heading.

Ron could only imagine what lurked in this country. He'd never been this far west, having come to Nevada less than a month ago in pursuit of his brother's killer. California had been a possible destination in the future, though it would have been a more defined route, for certain. These twisty woodland paths could lead anywhere, and it wasn't nice being whacked in the face by limbs at every turn.

They stopped to rest the horses shortly after noon, in a small clearing with green grass and a swampy patch where Joella dug a hole and refilled her canteens. She was kind enough to offer Ron a drink, which he gladly took, for he hadn't quenched his thirst since the kidnapping. The liquid soothed his parched throat and let him breathe a sight easier. All he needed now was a good meal, though he didn't feel there was a point in asking. His captor wasn't eating, so it was doubtful she'd waste rations on him.

Once Ron had drunk his fill, Joella refilled the canteens again and tied her captive to one of the grazing horses, after which she disappeared into the bushes.

Alone for the first time, Ron saw his opportunity to escape. The sturdy ropes around his wrists may have been tied securely, but this wasn't the first time he'd had to escape from captivity. His hands could be deceptive, for while they looked fat and chubby, they were scarcely wider than his wrists. With the right moves, he could be free!

While drinking, he'd been clever enough to leak a bit of the water down his hands and wrists, wetting the rope and lubricating his dry skin. Sliding his wrists back and forth inside the wet rope, he managed to loosen it the tiniest margin. Then, tucking his thumb and fingers together, he was able to pull one hand through, and released his second with a quick pick of the remaining knot.

Ron made a dash for the swampy edge of the clearing. He figured it was his best bet for escape, as Joella wasn't liable to be lurking in that area. She'd entered the bushes on the opposite side of the clearing, and even if she'd circled around a bit, it was doubtful she'd be wading around in the mud.

He didn't get past the hole Joella had dug when his legs went numb. Instantly, the knees bent and Ron threw his arms out in front of him, barely able to stop from getting planted face-first in the muck. He sank almost to his elbows in the soft soil before the tingling hit his shoulders, causing him to collapse. As feeling left his arms, he managed to roll onto his side, and not get a mouthful of dirt when he fully collapsed.

He lay there for a few minutes before Joella finally returned.

"You can't get away from me that easily," Joella said as she approached the paralyzed dwarf.

"Think I wouldn't try?" Ron asked, his face half covered in crud.

"I was certain you would," Joella said, pulling his limp body out of the mossy muck. "It's good you've gotten it out of your system."

"Who says I have?" Ron said spitefully.

"The proximity tether I have latched onto you," Joella explained. "If you get too far away from me, it reactivates the dormant paralytic dust in your system. Don't try running again."

"You could've told me," Ron mentioned. "Would've saved you all the trouble of setting up this test of yours."

"It wasn't a test," Joella said, tossing him on the ground beside the horses. She untied the rope from the horse and began binding his wrists again.

"Then why duck off into the woods like that?"

"Why do you think? I had to refresh myself."

"Is that elf speak for taking a crap?"

"That's lady speak, you uncouth midge," Joella answered, tossing the dwarf onto the horse. "You've got a lot to learn, Boron Grimes."

"Says you," Ron answered bitterly.

With the afternoon sun lingering in the sky, their pace hastened as they came to better defined trails. Hour after hour, the signs of life grew more numerous. Several cabins came and went, and a few ploughed fields appeared as civilization returned. Near nightfall, a sizeable town could be seen in the distance, tucked into a valley surrounded by two streams that emptied into a small lake in the center.

"Welcome to Ravenna-West," Joella said as they crossed a log bridge at the edge of town.

Past the bridge, they rode straight down Main Street, a wide, dirt road with ruts full of gravel. Some of the locals were still out and about, and their physical features were plain to see, even in the gathering gloom. This was an elf town, for certain.

Most of the residents didn't pay them much mind, though Ron caught a few staring at him with dirty looks on their narrow faces. His stout form made him stand out like a sore thumb, even on horseback, and these people weren't much for outsiders.

Elves were a tricky lot to place, like any sentient race. Their customs and attitudes varied greatly by clan, though based on the location of Ravenna-West, Ron could make a guess about their proclivities. These were isolationists, seeking their own secluded life separate from the outside world. They might have dealings with the occasional trader, but it was doubtful they'd let any strangers set up shop in this neck of the woods.

Joella stopped their journey in front of a large, stone building in the center of town. The colorful stained glass windows revealed it to be an elvish temple, their central place of worship and governance. The building's circular shape and slate roofing made it stand out compared to the other buildings in town.

Joella dismounted and hastily untied the rope around Ron's wrists. "Follow me and do what I say, assuming you want to live," she commanded.

Ron said nothing, and continued to wonder about her current scheme as she led him into the round building.

Entering the small antechamber, Joella stopped in front of a large basin atop a pedestal and dipped two fingers into the clear liquid. She touched the damp fingers to her forehead and ordered Ron to do the same. Sticking his fingers into the bowl, he felt the oily substance soak into his skin, leaving a chilling nip. He didn't like the idea of rubbing the stuff on his sweaty brow, but felt he had no alternative, and did a quick swipe just as his captor had done. As the oil soaked in, it served to soothe his sun-burnt brow.

Joella stopped in front of two silvery, metal doors and pounded her fist against them. A few moments passed, and the doors creaked open, revealing the spacious chamber beyond. Curved pews were set in half rings, leading toward the back of the room, where a raised platform held a single occupant perched at a desk covered in books. His gaze was upon the two intruders as they walked toward him.

"High Minister," Joella greeted as she neared the elf on the platform.

"Widow Lafayette," the High Minister replied with an emotionless tone.

"I've returned with my husband's killer," Joella said.

"And I take it your intentions have not changed?" the High Minister asked, sounding hopeful to the contrary.

"They have not, High Minister."

The High Minister glanced at the ceiling and breathed a deep breath. "Very well, bring him to me."

Joella grabbed Ron's arm and dragged him onto the platform. Before releasing her grip, she whispered into his ear. "Be honest, and accept the consequences of your actions."

Ron felt a surge of apprehension pulse through his chest as he was pushed forward to face the High Minister.

"Confirm your name," the High Minister commanded.

"Boron Grimes," Ron replied nervously.

"Word has reached this court that a Boron Grimes did kill one of our clansmen, Vincent Lafayette. Are you that same man?"

"Yes," Ron said, unashamed.

"And this was done on the field of honor, in personal combat?"

"Yes."

"And it was done honorably, with no unnatural advantages or extraneous influences?"

"I killed him fair and square, if that's what you're asking," Ron replied.

"You swear to it?" the High Minister asked.

"I do," Ron said.

The High Minister sat silently, glaring at the short man in front of the desk. "My empathy reveals only truth to your words," he finally said, sounding disappointed. "Lafayette's death requires no retribution."

Ron felt relieved, assuming he was off the hook.

"High Minister," Joella interjected, stepping up to the desk. "You have confirmed that this man killed my husband on the field of honor. By Clan Law, I claim Widow's Rights."

"Truly, Widow Lafayette, do you wish to be so brash?"

Grabbing Ron's hand and yanking it forward, she said, "I have no choice."

"As widow, you have the right to claim restitution from your husband's killer. Do you wish to exercise that right?"

"I do," Joella said, shooting Ron a nasty stare.

Turning to Ron, the High Minister lowered his tone. "As an outsider to our clan and our race, you are free to renounce the widow's claim, and be exempted from our laws in this matter. If you so choose..."

"He accepts my claim," Joella interrupted. "Don't you, Grimes?" She squeezed his hand, digging her fingernails into his knuckles.

"Uh, yes," Ron said, heeding her previous advice. She'd threatened to kill him if he didn't comply with her wishes, and he was in no mood to test her resolve. Besides, he was morbidly curious to learn what these Widow's Rights entailed.

"So be it," the High Minister said. "Then by my authority as anointed spiritual leader of this Clan of Talus, I hereby assign all marital responsibilities of Vincent Lafayette to you, Boron Grimes."

"What?" Ron said, wondering if he'd heard right.

"You are hereby married, Mister and Misses Grimes," the High Minister said coldly.

"That's it?" Ron asked. "No wedding? No *'for sicker or poorer.'* No *'if anybody objects let them speak now or forever hold their peace?'*"

"No," the High Minister replied. "Under these circumstances, Widow Lafayette was well within her rights to claim your hand in marriage, as restitution for the death of her husband. This is our

Clan Law, as it has been practiced for thousands of years."

"What about divorce?" Ron asked, after which Joella slapped the back of his head.

"Again, it is at her sole discretion. You are married, Mr. Grimes, for better or worse, until death or until Mrs. Grimes-Talus chooses to release you."

"Which will not happen," Joella said, kneeling. Grabbing Ron by both cheeks, she kissed him briefly. "You are mine. Get used to it."

The High Minister pulled a form out of a desk drawer and began filling it out. The text of the document was in both English and Elavic, the ancient script of the Elvish Hierarchy. Once he had the empty slots filled, he handed it to Joella, who promptly signed it, then handed it to Ron, who reluctantly put his name to it.

"It is done," the High Minister said, adding his signature to the bottom. "I'll have this forwarded to Sacramento on our next mail run." After tucking the marriage license away, he removed another document and filled it out in haste. "Here's your proof, if anyone should ask."

"Thank you, High Minister," Joella said, taking the certificate from his grasp. "Come along, dear. Time for you to meet the in-laws."

Ron swallowed the growing lump in his throat, as the weight of the situation continued to fall. And he'd thought being indentured to Doliber would be a trial. How accursed to be shackled to an elf!

* * *

A cold drizzle was blowing in off the bay when Doliber arrived in San Francisco. He'd always hated it here, spending all those years at school, trying to hone his inherent mystic talents during the day, braving the bitter winds and bustling markets in his free time, unable to find satisfaction in so many respects. Why the Guild had chosen to locate their West American chapter in this god-awful city continued to elude him.

The cold was an added shock to his system, as he'd just teleported from an eighty-degree hotspot. Suddenly hitting that fifty degree mist would send a chill down anyone's back. The thin, leather coat helped a little, but he wasted no time getting indoors.

The Guildmaster's home was a modest, unsuspecting house on Fulton Street, a few blocks from the campus of the Guild's western academy.   The door knocker was the most impressive thing in sight, a solid brass lion without a spot of tarnish.   Three hard raps of the knocker announced Doliber's presence, and the door opened soon after, all by itself.

Stepping inside, Doliber removed his hat and coat, setting them on a nearby bench before heading inside.   As he moved to leave the entryway, a clear voice halted him.   "Aren't we forgetting something?"

Doliber grumbled in frustration as he sat down to remove his dusty boots.   He hadn't forgotten at all, but had tried to avoid the annoying practice.   Nothing got past the Guildmaster, however, so he had to accommodate the elder.

Once in his stocking feet, Doliber continued down the hall, reaching the Guildmaster's home office after two dozen steps.

The small room was half library, half reliquary, littered with mystic antiquities.   Among the carefully arranged items was a circular table with a globe in the center.   It was there that the aging Giuldmaster sat, flipping through the pages of a leather-bound reference book.

"So, Journeyman Doliber, what brings you to see me?" the Guildmaster asked, looking up from his text to stare at his guest.

"I suspect you know," Doliber replied, looking at the head of his mystic order.   The gray-haired man with a neatly-trimmed beard was getting fat in his latter years, though there was no sign of infirmity.   The bushy brow accentuated the fiery eyes that glared back, and the crow's-feet at the temples only added distinction.

Slapping the book shut, the Guildmaster replied, "I am aware of no such thing.   Please, enlighten me."

Doliber stormed up to the table and slapped his palms on the smooth surface.   "I'm investigating a robbery and a multiple homicide."

The Guildmaster sighed and shook his head.   "Oh, how boorish.   I thought you would have learned by now the folly of involving yourself in the affairs of the common people."

"I serve and protect society from those who would abuse and betray all that is good in this country."

"As a county sheriff? Please, don't elevate your position."

"Why do you rebuke me?" Doliber asked, frustrated.

"You were a prized pupil, once," the Guildmaster mentioned, reaching over and spinning the globe. "You were so talented, had such potential. It pains me to see your talents wasted."

"What would you have me do? Study in seclusion, ignoring the ills of this world? Shutting myself away like the rest of the Guild in pursuit of some spiritual truth? What would be the point of that?"

"The answer, former apprentice, is in the journey, or have you forgotten? Seeking truth is a purpose unto itself. Always learning, always expanding our understanding of the universe, those are the principles upon which our organization was founded, and to those we must adhere."

"I did not come here to rehash old grievances," Doliber said, feeling he'd been lectured enough.

"Then what is your intent?"

"The crimes I'm investigating concern the Guild."

"How could such a material matter pertain to us?"

"The perpetrator was a human mystic of significant skill, the sort of skill only taught by this organization."

The Guildmaster flinched at the statement, unprepared for the implications.

"That's right. A member of your precious Guild is a thief and a murderer," Doliber said, feeling cocky. "How does that align with your vaunted principles?"

"This is wholly unfathomable!" the Guildmaster cursed, leaping from his seat in a bout of controlled rage. "To think a member of our order capable of wanton acts of destruction..." Freezing in mid-sentence, he let his expression grow blank and locked his gaze onto Doliber. "Show me everything."

In the blink of an eye, Doliber's mind replayed the events for the Guildmaster, showing him the scene of the crime, the mutilated stagecoach, and the bloody bodies. All memory of the experience was relayed; sight, sound, touch, scent. The aged master was able to witness all that the sheriff had witnessed, as if he'd been there, himself.

As the last sensory information was transferred, the

Guildmaster blinked and sat down in silent contemplation.

Feeling a stinging aftershock from the experience, Doliber wiped his eyes and breathed a deep breath, fighting to clear his head. An ordinary mind reading would not have affected him so severely, but the invasive nature of the Guildmaster's scan staggered him. Even so, he refused to show weakness and remained on his feet as he recovered.

"This is most troubling," the Guildmaster said at last, rubbing his hairy chin. "The spell traces you perceived, they were certainly human, and not the work of any amateur. The skill required to harness such power requires very specialized training."

"The kind only the Guild can provide a man," Doliber stated.

"True, and power only a full master could possess."

Doliber saw a peculiar look in the Guildmaster's eye, and jumped on it. "You know who it is, don't you?"

"Nothing is certain," the Guildmaster rebutted. "I must confer with the other elders before saying more. You must go."

There was no point in arguing. Doliber had gotten all he would out of the man for the moment, as little as it was. He didn't like leaving empty handed, though.

"I'll see myself out," Doliber said as the Guildmaster stood to escort him.

Turning to leave, Doliber closed his eyes and sent his mind wandering. For a second that seemed like minutes, his consciousness floated outside his body, following the lingering ethereal trail left behind by the Guildmaster's previous intrusion. The magic tracks left the warlock with an opening into the master's mind, if he were strong enough to sneak through without detection. It was a trick few had ever attempted against such a powerful mystic, and one Doliber would never have dared to try, were the situation not so dire. Things were being concealed, and he had to know the truth!

His mind floated through the glowing realm of unseen magic, passing through the waves and ripples of mental essence. There, among the flow of light was a large patch of glistening life, and a hoard of mental data waiting to be explored; the body and soul of the Guildmaster. Looking at the shielded lump, Doliber detected several slender cracks in the armor, the lingering holes where the

Guildmaster had ventured beyond his own being mere moments ago. Those cracks could be used in reverse for a limited time, and Doliber wasted none. Throwing his discorporeal mind through the ether, he reached into the Guildmaster's mind, and gazed upon the surface.

The surge of information would prove overwhelming for your average human mind, and even Doliber found it troubling. The added thoughts and feelings of a second consciousness stunned him as he took it all in. The shock quickly severed his link, and left him staggering toward a wall.

Feeling the sting of the intrusion, the Guildmaster shook it off and growled. "Of all the insolent behavior!"

"I had to see your mind," Doliber defended, leaning against the doorframe. "Lives may depend on it."

The Guildmaster stormed over and stood in the doorway, so he could look at Doliber's face. "And what makes you the master of those lives?"

"The people who elected me to be their sheriff, that's who. It's my job."

"Yet you came to me for help, because you're out of your depth," the Guildmaster said. "Now you presume to take charge, steal my knowledge and venture into deeper water where you cannot swim!"

Doliber looked at the furious man, and felt the sting of his rebuke. This had been an underhanded path to take, and it hadn't been his intention to violate trust. There was genuine shame in his heart for behaving so brashly. "I'm sorry to disappoint you, again."

"Well, no real harm done," the Guildmaster said, regaining an amiable attitude. He walked back to his reading table and took a seat. "Still, I believe it is time you took your leave."

Feeling he'd done all he could, Doliber headed for the outside door. It was high time he got back to Selwood and continued his investigation. Pulling on his boots and grabbing his hat and coat, he reached for the knob, but before he could open the door to depart, the Guildmaster's voice called from down the hall.

"The knowledge you received from that ever so brief intrusion into my psyche is no doubt jumbled and fairly useless. If you'll take my advice, you'll leave it like that. Don't go picking through it to find bits of data that will only lead to confuse you further."

"Why?" Doliber asked, gripping the doorknob tightly. "What are you afraid I'll find?"

"Have patience, Journeyman Doliber. All will be revealed in due course. Return to your worldly duties, and I shall contact you shortly."

Doliber yanked the door open and went outside, back into the cold mist that had become a steady downpour. He didn't stick around to face the wet weather, and opted for a quick teleport back to Selwood, where a much greater storm was brewing.

The hot air greeted him like a kiss, as his body materialized on the porch in front of his office. This was where he belonged, in the arid world of prospectors and frontiersmen. Civilization was a bit too civilized for his liking, and his greatest concern was where he'd go next, if this wild corner of the world built up around him before he got old. He liked it here, and didn't want things to change.

Clomping up the steps to his office, twisted images continued to roll around inside his head, the jumbled memories of the Guildmaster. They were little more than phantoms, but Doliber knew the answers he sought had to be there. He needed time to meditate and rest before he could unlock the secrets he'd stolen.

Doliber stepped into his office, and listened to the silence. Things were pretty quiet around here for the moment. The holding cells in back were empty, and there weren't any rowdy cattlemen visiting town. Taking advantage of the peace, he turned to the slender flight of stairs near his desk, and headed for his bedroom on the second floor. It wasn't quite sunset, but near enough, and he had a lot of work to do.

As his head hit the pillow, Doliber wondered how his new deputy was settling in.

* * *

The warm afternoon sun was creeping toward the mountains on the western horizon as Ron Grimes followed his new wife out into the muddy street. He was still trying to wrap his head around the whole thing, and couldn't for the life of him explain it. He'd thought elves were bizarre before; now he thought them just plain nuts.

"Saddle up," Joella said, unhitching her horse. "It's time I introduced you to the rest of the family."

"I don't get you," Ron said, jumping to catch the stirrup. "You kidnap me, haul me all this way, just to get married?"

"I had no choice," Joella said, sounding ashamed. It was the first sign of gentler emotions she'd revealed in Ron's presence. "Ride. I'll explain along the way."

Getting onto the horse, Ron squirmed as he tried to position himself. The thing didn't feel right. The saddle was designed for someone with longer legs and broader hips, and as the steed began trotting along, the hard leather pounded his tail bone in a most sinister manner. He hadn't noticed it so much while he was a prisoner, but now that he was riding without ropes around his wrists, he had more attention to focus on minor discomforts. She could have at least kidnapped him with his own horse!

Joella led the way out of town, down a well traveled dirt road heading north. The muddy fields of hay and wheat stubble buttressed either side of the ruts, and further along cattle could be seen in fenced pastures. The hilly ground hid the farm houses that lurked amongst the agricultural lands. It was several miles before trees once again appeared, and Joella decided to speak.

"Tell me, Dwarf, how do your people court a mate?"

Ron scoffed at the direct question, thinking the answer to be pretty obvious. "How do you figure? If a guy likes a girl, he takes her out to a show or dinner, buys her pretty gifts; stuff like that. Why?"

Joella looked over her shoulder and gave him a funny look. "You clearly haven't been around elves before, at least none who adhere to clan traditions. In our society, courtship is a formality, practiced only by those men who choose to be chivalrous. You see, we don't choose our mates. Our parents do."

"Arranged marriages are nothing new," Ron mentioned.

"No, they're very old. Archaic, I'd say, but the clans have two thousand years of precedence on their side, and most elves like the way things are. So, we stick with a backwards system which treats women like property, and marriage to be a legal contract devoid of emotional considerations."

"What's all this got to do with you marrying me?" Ron asked, nudging his horse to catch up with hers. Once they were side-by-side, he could get a good look at her face as she replied.

"It was my way out. When you killed my husband—a husband I was betrothed to at birth—you gave me the rare opportunity to get away from these legally-imposed marriages. Since you killed Vincent honorably in a duel, I had the Widow's Right to claim you for my husband."

"What would've happened if we hadn't gotten hitched?" Ron asked.

"Then I'd become the responsibility of Vincent's next of kin, who could then claim me as a wife, or marry me off to one of his cousins. I'd have no say in the matter, so you can understand why I had to do this."

Ron shook his head in disgust. It hadn't been so long ago, there'd been a war fought over slavery, and a Constitutional Amendment ratified to end it forever. Yet, out here, among the various clans and religious sects of the frontier, he'd seen far too much of the practice. Always veiled under another title and justified by tradition, but it was still slavery. He couldn't escape the belief that society would always be cursed with the scourge, in one form or another.

"Don't feel so bad, Mister Grimes. Play your cards right and you won't have to put up with me too long—just until we get your new in-laws off our collective backs."

It was a great relief to hear, and for the first time in days Ron was feeling optimistic about things. This little sham marriage was a minor inconvenience, one that had the unintended consequence of prying him from Sheriff Doliber's grip. This was well outside the Sheriff's jurisdiction, so when Joella's plans were complete, he'd be a free man. Selwood was no place he'd miss, and there was plenty of wilderness to explore.

Sliding a hand down his side instinctively, Ron recalled one important element that was missing. "Say, what'd you do with my Remington?" he asked his new wife.

"That clunky old cap and ball thing you had? I left it at the bar in Selwood. Why?"

Damn! Just when he'd thought he was free and clear, this pointy-eared broad had to go and leave the one thing he cared about back in that dust trap of a town. Would it even be there if he went back for it? There was no telling what that lousy barkeeper would do with it, but Ron was sure going to find out.

Of course, that would have to wait until his dear wife let him go. When that would be was anyone's guess.

A fork in the road appeared, and Joella led them to the right, up a slight slope. The gradual incline decreased after a few hundred yards, and turning a corner revealed a house with white clapboards surrounded by a modest lawn and spacious fields beyond. There was something well-to-do about the place, and it was obviously not your average ranch.

As Ron and Joella neared the lawn, the front door of the house opened, and a lady in white dress stepped out onto the porch.

"Who's that?" Ron asked as Joella climbed down off her horse.

"Mehitable Sellius-Vellinar, first wife of Mactus Sellius."

"And that means?"

"Mactus is Vincent Lafayette's first cousin, his closest blood relative and would-be inheritor. If I hadn't married you, I'd be his, to do with as he pleased. I'm a Talus, so he'd love nothing better than to marry me."

"Yeah, but he's already got a wife," Ron said, planting his feet on the grassy ground. It was quite a drop from the horse for the dwarf, but his legs still had a good spring in them.

"He already has three," Joella corrected. "Two through marriages arranged before his fifth birthday, another through *other* means. I had no intention of being wife number four in his little harem. Understand?"

"I'm starting to," Ron said. It was finally clear why an elf would stoop so low as to marry a dreaded "midge."

With a spry and confident stride, Joella walked up onto the uncovered porch. Ron waited at the base of the steps, wondering how this was going to go down.

"Hello, Hittie," Joella greeted the elf woman standing by the door. "How have you been?"

"Why, just fine, Widow Lafayette," Hittie replied cordially. From her tone of voice and the youthful looks, Ron guessed her age at about twenty, though elves were notorious for their young appearances, even into old age, so she could be much older.

"I'm here to see Mactus," Joella said. "May I come in?"

"Of course. We've been expecting you," Hittie said sweetly. "I'm afraid Mactus isn't here right now, but he should be back soon. If you'd like to put your feet up for a spell, I'm sure he'll be along any time. Then we can get you all dressed up for the big day. We'll have to fit you with a new dress, and find you some decent jewelry. The other wives will no doubt want to donate an item or two. Will that be all right?"

"How kind of you," Joella said, placing a hand on Hittie's shoulder. "To think you and Mactus would go to all that trouble to celebrate my wedding."

"Well, of course we are, dear. You deserve your proper day."

"Yes, I suppose I do," Joella said, fighting back an amused smile. She clearly enjoyed toying with the woman, playing on her ignorance of the situation.

"Now, come on inside. I've got a fresh pot of that parsnip stew, just like your grandma used to make for Sunday socials."

Joella took a step inside the door and turned to Ron. "Coming, sweetie?"

Ron frowned at her playful demeanor but stepped forward. As he neared the door, Hittie finally acknowledged his existence.

"Excuse me, dear, what is this?" she asked rudely.

"This is my new husband," Joella said with a straight face. "I thought you knew."

"Boron Grimes, ma'am," Ron said, offering his hand.

"What?" Hittie exclaimed. "Surely, you can't be serious."

"He killed Vincent in an honorable duel, so I exercised my Widow's Rights accordingly. You do understand."

Hittie froze with a vacant look on her face. Her wide eyes followed Ron as he walked inside and caught up to Joella.

"Come along, husband," Joella said as she proceeded down the hall. "We don't want our stew to get cold."

Ron followed, shaking his head in disbelief.

Episode Three:
Marriage of Inconvenience

A pair of elvish riders came trotting into Ravenna-West near dusk, with a western breeze on their backs. The final merchants who were closing up shop for the day took notice of the two men and gave them a conciliatory nod in passing. Both men were well known in these parts, the wealthy and powerful Sellius brothers.

Mactus Sellius was portly for an elf, a byproduct of his affluence and eating habits. By contrast, his brother Gregory was your typical beanpole of elvish form, fit and trim from both behavior and good breeding. Both men wore matching gray suits, and still looked well kept, even after a week on the trail.

The Sellius brothers hitched their horses in front of the temple, and proceeded inside to speak with the High Minister. Mactus pounded a summons on the door, and tapped his foot against the floor as he waited for a response. Before long, the door creaked open and a head peeked out.

"Ebenezer, my friend," Mactus said familiarly as the High Minister opened the door. "How have you been?"

High Minister Ebenezer Fallios didn't look happy, and replied in a morose tone. "We have a problem." He stepped aside and invited the men to enter.

Mactus and Gregory followed Ebenezer into his private office, a well ordered room behind the cluttered reception chamber. The place had all the comforts of modern living, including patent-leather chairs and a private bar. This was a room familiar to the Sellius brothers, and they took their regular seats around a crystal coffee table.

"So, what seems to be the problem, and what can we do to rectify it?" Mactus asked.

Before responding, Ebenezer pulled a bottle of aged brandy from the shelf and poured drinks for his guests. Handing over the large snifters, he said, "The Widow Lafayette's the problem."

"Oh, *that* problem," Mactus said with amusement. "Well, we'll soon fix that, won't we? Haven't you drafted the marriage license yet?"

"Indeed, I have," Ebenezer answered, sitting down without a glass. He was rarely one to drink, though he enjoyed the company of those who did. "Our problem is the groom."

"I don't see the problem," Mactus answered after a slurp from the glass. "Vincent Lafayette was my first cousin. He had no closer relations, therefore I inherit."

"Unless," Ebenezer prompted.

"Unless what? She invokes Widow's Rights? Vint was shot by a filthy midge. Unless she intends to marry..." He trailed off as he saw the High Minister nodding.

A chilling silence fell upon the room.

"What are you saying?" Gregory finally spoke. "That Joella actually intends to get hitched to a dwarf?"

"I'm afraid it has gone beyond intent," Ebenezer replied. "Joella invoked her Widow's Rights this very day."

"What?" Mactus shouted, jumping to his feet, enraged. "How could you let this happen? Do you realize what you've done?"

"Calm down," Ebenezer commanded in a stern voice. "You know the law. I had no choice but to fulfill her wishes."

Mactus wiped a hand over his pudgy face and sat down, considering the full weight of the situation. He took another large sip of the brandy and let his imagination wander to lewd images of his would-be bride, the widow of his aunt's son. His thoughts quickly betrayed him, as a vision of her coupling with a dirt covered dwarf filled his mind. He knew little about the dwarf, so his own prejudice created a hairy, snarling beast tackling Joella like a wild animal. How revolting, yet strangely arousing! Mactus shivered in response to his conflicting emotions and downed the last of his drink.

"Do you require a refill?" Ebenezer asked, taking the empty snifter.

"Yes," Mactus replied.

"This is insane," Gregory said. "To think any elf, let alone someone of Joella's breeding, would lower herself to couple with a dwarf. It's unconscionable."

"That woman hates me," Mactus said after downing half of his second glass. "Didn't think she'd go this far to spite me." He followed his words with the rest of his drink, which provided a comforting glaze over his eyes. He let the familiar feeling of inebriation sink in, hoping it would take the emotional sting away. Somehow, it wasn't working, and after the High Minister poured him a third glass, he let it sit, untouched.

"I'm sorry, Mactus, I really am," Ebenezer said, sitting down after playing waiter to his guest.

Gregory was still nursing his first glass of booze, seeming more interested in talking through the situation. "Can't believe any self respecting elf could get hitched to a midge. It's bad enough when they dilute the gene pool with those lousy humans. Just 'cause you *can* breed with something doesn't mean you should."

"Yeah, our no good cousin Vint was proof of that," Mactus said, touching his full snifter, but restraining himself. "Damn half-breeds will be the death of our society. What kind of law invites our own extermination?"

"It's hardly that bad," Ebenezer replied calmly. "Clan Law has permitted the intermarrying of humans and dwarves with our kind for centuries. It's rarely done, for obvious reasons, but freedom of choice was the Grand Council's intention all those years ago. It is not for you or I to question the law, merely to abide by it."

"Even if the Clan Chieftain's heir hooks up with a midge?" Gregory asked, swishing the liquid in his glass.

"Even then," Ebenezer mentioned. "It's not like the title has any meaning these days. This is America. We aren't ruled by chieftains or monarchs anymore."

"You damn well know it still means something," Mactus grumbled in his half-drunken state. "All the ancestral heirs retain a lot of influence and power, just 'cause of who they are."

"Well, maybe that will change now that Joella has—as you so

aptly put it—married a filthy midge?" Ebenezer added. "Perhaps then more people will realize we aren't in the old country anymore."

"That's not the point," Mactus snapped. "Joella did this because of me, to spite *me!* The one woman who should've been mine all along, and what does she go and do? The unthinkable, that's what. It's personal, and I won't just sit by while she uses legal loopholes to spit on our traditions and laugh in my face. There has to be a way around this, Eb. Tell me there's a way."

"I'm sorry, but the marriage is iron-clad," Ebenezer replied. "I telegraphed Sacramento an hour ago with the particulars, and the official registration receipt will be sent out with the next mail runner. You'll simply have to accept that she beat you."

"Nobody beats Mactus Aaron Sellius!" He smacked the drink off the table, splashing the contents on the smooth hardwood floor. Amazingly, the glass landed unharmed.

"Calm down, Mactus," Ebenezer said, getting up to retrieve the fallen snifter and mop up the mess. After grabbing the glass, he found a spare towel behind the bar and wiped up the sprayed liquor.

"There's got to be a way," Mactus said.

"We could always shoot him," Gregory suggested.

The words hit Mactus like a lightning bolt. "Of course!" he exclaimed, snapping his fingers.

"What are you thinking, Mactus?" Ebenezer asked after a short silence.

"That dirty midge got Joella for killing my cousin. Seems only fair I get her the same way."

"You can't be serious," Ebenezer replied.

"Oh, I'm dead serious," Mactus rebutted. He tapped his brother on the shoulder and headed for the door. "I'm gonna deal with that midge, just like he did my cousin. Then, Joella will have no choice but to marry me."

"Where are you going?" Ebenezer asked.

"Back home, to get ready. There's gonna be a duel!"

* * *

Ron Grimes hated parsnips. The stringy white tubers resembling emaciated carrots had always disgusted him. His mother had learned early on to forego their preparation, but now he sat at this dining table with a steaming bowl of stew saturated in parsnip pulp. It was just the latest in a long line of indignities these lousy elves had bestowed upon him.

Joella smiled back at him from across the table, pleased with herself and the warm meal in front of her. The dull glow of the oil lamp exemplified the contrast between her dark hair and pale skin, giving her a ghostly appearance. She was very picturesque indeed, like something out of an old painting.

"Eat up, husband," Joella said, dipping her spoon into her bowl. "Don't want it getting cold."

"Yeah, it would be a real tragedy," Ron replied, fiddling with the sticky glop, but unwilling to taste it. He hadn't eaten the vile parsnip as a child, so why would he do so now? There had to be a way out of this. The right words of distraction could do the trick, though Ron wasn't the talkative type. His personality left him at a disadvantage, especially in the presence of a lady.

"Oh, come on," Joella said, sensing his aversion to the meal. "It's delicious."

He was being called out, so he had to speak up. "Nothing personal, but I'm not gonna eat this slop." He gently slid the bowl away from him.

Joella smiled, and the angle of the lighting made her look wicked. "All the more for me." Grabbing his bowl and setting it beside hers, she added, "Fine, don't eat. You could use to lose a few pounds, anyway."

"What's that supposed to mean?" Ron asked.

"You're round, Boron. While we're at it, would it kill you to use a razor? That beard makes you look like a goat."

"I haven't cut this face in three years, ain't gonna anytime soon," he exclaimed.

"And we'll have to do something about this guttural slang you seem to use whenever you're upset," Joella chided. "I can't have my husband saying *'ain't gonna'* all around town. What will people think?"

"That you married a dirty midge, that's what," Ron grumbled, wondering how much she meant, and how much was merely an act. They were in the lion's den here, masquerading as happily married in front of her former in-laws. Of course, she had to behave as she was; pretentious and eager to mould her new husband into something an elvish matron would desire. It was for that reason only, and the hope that he'd be a free man after this little visit, that made him bite his tongue. Even so, he couldn't help but consider some sort of payback in the future.

"Now, don't act like that, Boron. You know you're far too good a man to be called a midge," she said, sounding as if she believed it.

"Call me Ron," he mumbled.

"What?"

"Call me Ron," he said a little louder, but just barely enough for her to hear. "It's what my friends call me, what few of them I've got. Figure my wife ought to call me the same."

"Okay, Ron," Joella said, returning her attention to her stew. The room was warm, heated by the large cook stove in the adjoining kitchen, so the food hadn't cooled much during their little exchange. She hurried to finish the first bowl before turning to the one discarded by the dwarf.

Joella was an elegant eater. Ron watched her lift the spoon in rhythmic fashion from the bowl to her lips, and saw the food quickly vanish. With the meal consumed, she stacked one bowl inside the other and grinned with satisfaction.

"Eat like that, and you'll turn into a parsnip," a new voice said, breaking the silence.

Joella's eyes rose at the sound of the familiar voice. "Doreen?"

Ron glanced over his shoulder to see a slender elvish woman wearing a blue dress with pink frills. His scrutinizing eyes saw an immediate resemblance to Joella, though this woman was clearly older, with a few wrinkles starting above her eyebrow. The calluses on her hands and the dirt under her fingernails showed she was no stranger to labor, either. You had to give the elves credit; they knew how to work.

Joella stood up from her seat and hurried across the room to give Doreen a hug. "Ron, this is my first cousin, Doreen Sellius-Talus."

Ron gave a slight nod in recognition, remaining reserved. He continued to feel uncomfortable among the elves, and as he observed Joella and Doreen's exchange, questions plagued him. Their ways and behaviors were very alien, and he'd never given their species much thought because of it. Now, thrown headlong into their world, forced to be a prisoner of their customs, he couldn't put them out of his mind as usual. He thought it best to keep silent, to avoid any social faux pas.

"Have you heard the news?" Joella asked.

"Hittie just finished telling us in that emphatic way of hers," Doreen replied. "I don't know how she'll ever get over it. I think she was really looking forward to having you as a marriage-sister."

Joella made a dubious face which left both ladies laughing.

The dynamics of elvish relationships were still sinking in for Ron, and he didn't know whether he should be repulsed or enticed by the unusual arrangement. Dwarves were traditionally a monogamous people, and infidelity was strictly frowned upon. After such a puritanical upbringing, a man couldn't help but cling to a moral ethos.

"So, how are the children?" Joella asked after the laughing subsided.

"They're all just fine," Doreen replied. "Willow learned to walk recently, and Dorcas can already count to one hundred. It seems just last week Dorc was..."

Ron couldn't contain himself and started laughing.

"What's so funny?" Doreen asked.

"Leave it to an elf to name their kid *Dorcas*," Ron said in between chuckles.

Doreen's face turned upside down in an instant. "Dorcas was my mother's name, and her mother's before that."

"Gee, I'm sorry," Ron said, unable to stop his laughing.

"How dare you come into my house and spit on my heritage, you... you..."

"Calm down, Doreen," Joella urged, hoping to avoid further upset. "There's no offense intended. Ron's just from a different culture, that's all. I'm sure we'd find many of his family names ridiculous, as well."

Doreen stood rigidly and swallowed her anger. After a few deep breaths, she replied, "Oh, Jo, have you always been such a diplomat?"

"Not really. I just call it as I see it," Joella said. "Besides, I can't have you beating up my new husband, can I?"

"I'd let you beat up mine," Doreen said, only half joking.

"A tempting offer, but no. I think I've beaten him enough for one day."

"I'd say so," Doreen replied shooting Ron a quick sneer. "Honestly, I don't think anyone but you would go so far to avoid marrying Mactus. He is a pig, but in all fairness there are worse choices."

Joella looked at Ron and back at Doreen, thinking on her words. Mactus Sellius indeed was a pig, in the mental sense, and his waist line was slowly expanding to match that of his ego. But in this wild frontier that elves and men were taming, he was an influential soul, with wealth and prestige that would reflect well on his heirs. There was a definite allure to being a part of his family, though Joella had never wanted anything from the man. Her temperament was more akin to her dead husband, the outlaw, only differentially focused. She could never settle for being the dutiful wife of a social climber.

Still, hooking up with a dwarf was an extreme measure, one only the boldest of elvish ladies would consider, and one only Joella herself could actually go through with.

Being tethered to a half breed like Vincent Lafayette was one thing, sharing her life with a midge was another. She had never intended this to be a true coupling, only a means to an end. Yet, how far would she really have to go? Clan Law stipulated a true marriage couldn't exist without physical intimacy, and if anyone suspected her true intentions they might seek to have her marriage to Ron annulled. Considering how reluctant the High Minister had been to grant her Widow's Rights, it was doubtful he'd hesitate to exercise any escape clause. All he'd need is someone like Mactus to press the issue.

Joella may have been many things, but she was no prostitute. She would not sleep with a man for personal gain, if that were all it entailed. So, could she truly bring herself to share this dwarf's bed, solely as a means to an end?

The consequences of her actions were still sinking in, and she wondered if she could play it far enough to dispel the scrutiny of her fellow elves before discarding this little man.

Doreen spotted the pained look on Joella's face, and utilizing her inherent mystic talents, she performed a quick empathic scan. Her cousin's emotions were guarded, but not invisible to a high-level empath; not when such emotions were brought to the surface by deep contemplation. The truth Doreen had suspected all along was instantly spelled out for her, and she knew it was urgent that she not let anyone else learn what she'd seen.

Grabbing Joella by the shoulders, Doreen turned her face away from the open hallway. "Careful," she whispered. "Can't let Hittie or Yuba spot that worry in your eyes."

"Worry? Me? What ever could I be afraid of?" Joella said, snapping back to her happy façade as she sat down beside Ron. She draped her left arm over his strong shoulders and gave him a ceremonious squeeze.

"Just keep your mental defenses up," Doreen cautioned. "And whatever you do, don't spend the night under this roof. Those two marriage sisters of mine can get pretty nosy, if you know what I mean."

Joella nodded, reading between the lines. "Thanks for the warning," Joella said loudly. "Ron and I certainly wouldn't want company on our wedding night."

All elves had a certain level of latent mystic ability, but how each elf developed their talents differed. Telepathic abilities were fairly common amongst the Talus clan, though there were unspoken rules which generally prevented unwarranted readings. It could be a handy thing to call for help in a pinch, or read the truth behind a child's confession, though digging into a person's thoughts unawares was generally taboo.

Remote viewing was another handy trick many elvish matrons learned. The ability to spy on their husbands, or watch their children in their heads from a distance was even more important than reading minds. It could also be abused for voyeuristic purposes, which could certainly threaten Joella's sham marriage.

Joella didn't have much in the way of magical powers. Her temperament wasn't geared toward their application, though she had picked up some impressive defensive tricks. Most of the time, she could shield her mind from intrusion, though she had to be conscious to do it, and her powers could do nothing to block a remote viewing. She wasn't going to risk that any of Mactus' family held such powers and was willing to use them against her.

Still, there was no sense making a run for it. That would look suspicious.

Once Joella's nerves steadied, she took Ron to meet the rest of her former in-laws. There was a spacious living room on the far side of the house, where the wives and children of Mactus congregated after nightfall. A fire raged in the large, stone fireplace, and oil lamps hung on the walls provided a dull but even light. Hittie played a few songs on the piano, and Doreen led everyone in chorus. Afterwards, Yuba, the third wife, read a fairy tale about elvish knights outwitting trolls and goblins in a medieval campaign. The six children were surprisingly even tempered, and stayed on their best behavior in front of the guests.

Through it all, Joella put on a happy face, and Ron sat quietly, waiting to escape.

As the hour grew late, and the children went off to bed, Joella finally decided to depart. Grabbing Ron by the hand and marching for the door, she bid the ladies farewell. She'd accomplished her goal, and was convinced it would be enough to keep Mactus off her back. Legally, she was free of him, and it was all the better that his family would be the ones to tell him, so she wouldn't have to face his outrage. At least, that was the plan.

As Joella and Ron stepped out into the night, a pair of riders came into the yard. The moon was in its first quarter, providing for limited vision, though it wasn't hard for Joella to identify the men. It was Mactus and that no good brother of his, Gregory.

When the horses came to a stop in front of the house, Mactus hopped down with a graceless thump. Handing the reigns to his brother, he ordered the skinny man to store the beasts in the barn. Then the portly elf swaggered toward the door, failing to notice the two people standing there until he nearly bumped into them.

"Hello, Mactus," Joella greeted as the man locked eyes with her.

"You treacherous hussy!" Mactus growled, covering his surprise with anger. "You dare show your face at my doorstep? Ah, it's just as well. Saves me the trouble of hunting you down."

"My *husband* and I were just leaving," Joella said, taking a step forward. Mactus blocked her way with an outstretched arm.

"I never believed you'd go this far. You shame yourself, and disgrace the entire clan with this action! I won't let you do it!"

"You're too late, Mactus," Joella said. "I'm already married, and there's nothing you can do about it." Without another word, she brushed by him, pulling Ron along by the arm. They were at their horses by the fence before Mactus shouted a response.

"Boron Grimes, I'm calling you out!"

Ron froze in mid-step and glanced over his shoulder, being careful not to make any sudden moves. The fat elf was standing there in the darkness, silhouetted in the faint moonlight, clearly ready to draw. "You don't want to do that," Ron warned.

"Don't tell me what I want!" Mactus shouted. "You think you can steal Joella from me? You've got another thing coming."

"I was never yours, Mactus," Joella rebutted. "He didn't steal me, so you have no legal grounds to challenge him."

"Don't I?" Mactus barked. "You are the chieftain's heir, and leadership of the clan shall pass to your children someday. If this dwarf would dare to marry you, seeking to be the father of that lineage, it is an insult to the entire Clan Talus, and I take that as grounds for a fight."

"Stop it!" Joella screamed storming over to Mactus and shoving him. "We're not in the old country. Clan Talus hasn't been for centuries, and we don't have a chieftain anymore."

"Maybe not now, but your bloodline still holds a lot of influence, and someday this clan will return to the old ways. When that day comes, I'll not have our chieftain be a filthy half-breed!"

Joella slapped him across the face with the back of her hand. "How dare you suggest we bow down to hereditary rulers! We're Americans, for God sake."

Mactus responded to Joella's blow in kind, smacking her hard with the palm of his hand. The stinging slap was powerful enough to send her staggering to the side. Ron shouted in protest, to which Mactus tossed back his jacket and placed a hand on the butt of his pistol. "Go ahead, little man. Draw!"

Ron felt inclined to oblige, but found himself at a disadvantage. "I'm not even armed," he admitted, hoping his foe would remain constrained by his code of honor.

Mactus grumbled and stomped his foot. "Well, damn it, get armed! Gregory! Where are you? Get back here and give this midge a gun!"

As they waited for Gregory to arrive, Doreen and Hittie came out to see what the commotion was about, which further fueled Mactus' frustration. He shouted for them to get inside, lest they accidentally catch a bullet when the duel started.

"Damn it, Mac, you're drunk," Doreen complained, smelling the booze on him from the doorstep. He was a good ten paces from the house, but the scent of his breath carried in the calm night air.

"Still sober enough to dispatch this worthless runt and claim Joella fair and square," Mactus said, his words sharp and clear despite his drinking.

"It's too dark, Mactus," Hittie said, sounding scared.

"Then light it up, Mehitable," Mactus replied, exasperated.

After shaking her head and sighing, Hittie did as he asked, extending her hand and focusing her gaze upon the night sky. After a moment of intense concentration, a beam of light streaked out of her hand and puffed out like a cloud above the front yard. The luminous fog hovered overhead, allowing clear vision within fifty yards of the house. It wasn't as strong as broad daylight, but certainly enough for a gunfight.

Mactus fidgeted, and wiped at his sweaty forehead several times as he waited for his brother to return from the stable. It wasn't a hot night, but nerves had a way of making a man perspire, as did the alcohol he'd been imbibing. It all left the elf drying his palms on his cotton jacket.

Gregory finally returned from stabling the horses and looked over the situation. He hadn't heard his brother yell for him, and wondered what the commotion was all about as he came into the glow of the mystic light.

"Throw the midge your gun," Mactus commanded urgently.

Always the dutiful little brother, Gregory did as he was asked, removing his pistol belt and tossing it to the dwarf. He knew what was afoot, and promptly stepped off to the side, wishing to avoid errant gunfire.

Looking back at his wives, Mactus snapped, "Get back in the house. Don't want the runt to clip either of you with his last bullet."

Hittie obeyed as the dutiful wife that she was, but Doreen refused, instead joining Gregory at the sidelines.

Taking a few steps forward, Mactus readied himself for the showdown.

"Don't do this, Mactus," Joella said, offering him a final out. "This is the man who shot Vincent Lafayette."

"Vint was a tenderfoot," Mactus snapped back, keeping his eyes locked on his intended target. "Everyone knows it. The only reason I never dusted him is he never gave me just cause. Gregory, count us down!"

The count started at five, and Ron felt time slow around him, as if the hands of time were covered in a thick frost. Each word ticked by as he stood there, clinging to the strange revolver in his hand, feeling the moment approaching. Each heart beat followed the countdown, as his five senses merged into one.

This was a familiar sensation, though not a frequent one. Gunfighting wasn't Ron's choice; though he wasn't afraid to use his inherent skills when the opportunity arose. He couldn't help being good at it. He simply was.

Gregory uttered *one*, and the pistols were whipped from their holsters. Ron lifted the Colt up to chest level, cocked the hammer with the palm of his left hand, and pulled the trigger with his right forefinger, all in one swift, fluid motion. He didn't think about it, acting purely on instinct. As the cloud of white smoke flowed up into his face from the pistol's barrel, his senses separated again, and his perceptions returned to normal, finding he was very much alive and unwounded.

"Mac!" a voice shouted, and Ron turned to see Gregory rushing over to his brother, who was floundering around on the ground.

Keeping out of the way, Joella nudged Doreen in the side. "Hey, looks like we might be marriage sisters, after all," she quipped.

Doreen clearly didn't appreciate the joke and stood silently, looking on.

Gregory dropped to his knees and cradled Mactus in his arms.

The bleeding was plainly visible as Ron approached, but it was hardly a lethal wound. The bullet had gone clean through the elf's shoulder.

"You're lucky I didn't have my Remington," Ron said, tossing the unfamiliar Colt at Mactus' feet. "Damn thing pulls high and to the right."

"I can't believe it," Mactus uttered, as his brother helped him up.

"Your *'affair of honor'* is finished," Ron chided. "I won, you lost, get over it. Accept that Joella's mine, and be glad you're still alive. Now, put some pressure on that wound before you bleed to death."

Ron turned and walked back to Joella, who was waiting by their horses, alone. "Where'd Doreen go?"

"Off," was all that Joella said, as she untied her horse from the hitching rail. "Come on, let's get out of here before there's any more trouble."

As Ron hopped on his horse and turned it toward the main road, Mactus shouted, "I'll get you for this, Grimes! By God, you've not seen the last of me!"

"Maybe not," Ron said, trotting past the obstinate elf, "but if you try anything stupid like this again, it is God you'll be seeing."

Ron nudged his horse into a full gallop, smiling all the while as he caught up with Joella. Maybe being chained to an elf wouldn't be so bad after all?

Episode Four:
Into the Thick of It

The cavern was spacious. For thousands of years, an underground river had cut through the rock, eating away at the sandstone composites, exposing the lines of petrified sediment in all their beauty. The water had not given any thought to what it was doing; as a power of nature, it had simply done what the laws of physics had designed it to do, flow toward the pull of gravity, seeking rest.

Tobias Sylvestri, the warlock in black, smiled as he entered the cavern, wondering if people were not the same in the grand scheme of things. How did their action differ from that of the water? Conscious awareness did little to change the hand of fate, and man's actions were generally predictable, following the path of least resistance. If one could give the water a mind to think, would it change direction, or would it keep doing what it had always done, and eat away at the rock?

Such ponderings were better left to the hereafter, as they confounded the mind of mortal man, though some were not given the luxury of ignorance.

"It is good you have returned to me so quickly, my son," a gravelly voice echoed around the room.

"I'm not your son," Tobias replied, incensed by the comment.

"Of course," the voice replied in conciliation. "Come forth."

Tobias moved forward along the smooth floor of the cavern. While the walls retained their natural shape, as carved by millennia of water, the base of this passage was artificially cut. The gloss of the floor reflected the magical lighting overhead, revealing a myriad of red and brown streaks of the polished rock. Despite the smoothness, there was good traction as well, and Tobias made his way forward, until he turned a corner and the chasm opened up into a wide expanse.

The new section of cave appeared as a great audience hall, with rows of pews leading up to a crystal throne. The walls had tapestries draped here and there, often depicting some grand battle or landscape. The most knowledgeable scholars could positively identify this chamber as an audience hall of the Wuertmost Goblins, though its location would prove baffling. The Wuertmost had gone extinct almost a thousand years ago, in lower Germany. Their presence on the North American continent was not even suspected, yet here it was, a perfectly preserved relic from a fallen realm.

In front of the throne was a large table covered with tools and trinkets, and an old man stood there picking through it all. He kept his attention fixated on a particular piece as the warlock approached.

"I've brought the gold you requested, Sage," Tobias said, stepping up to the old man, who continued to ignore him.

"I know," the old man said, keeping his attention on a strange plate of metal. It was unlike anything the warlock had seen before, a green sheet with golden streaks running in jagged lines across both sides. "What of the *other* item?"

"I have it here," Tobias said, tapping his chest pocket on his coat. He handed the pewter box to the sage, who grabbed it with great zest.

The Sage furrowed his brow as he looked over the closed container. Looking straight into Tobias' eyes, he snapped, "You opened the box!"

"You didn't really expect me to deliver it sight unseen, did you?" he admitted, seeing no point in hiding the fact now that he'd been caught.

"Those were your instructions," the sage said sternly.

"Look, I did what you wanted. I robbed the coach, stole the gold, and took this little metal box they had in the safe's hidden compartment. Ferguson and Finney went to all that trouble to hide it, and you wanted it so badly, I had to know what it was that everybody was so keen on acquiring. Can't imagine what you want with some hunk of gray metal."

Without warning, an invisible force slammed Tobias in the face, sending him hurtling across the room. The mystical blow left him momentarily stunned, but he was no pushover. With a quick thought, he activated a counterspell, and brought himself to a halt in the middle of the room. He staggered to his feet, grabbing the back of a pew for support.

"You pathetic child! Do you have any idea what you've exposed yourself to? There's enough radiation in that hunk of ore to rot your guts out before the year is through!"

Tobias marched back to the table and the imposing sage. "Look, I don't know anything about this rat attrition, but I know a mystic hex when I see one. Don't worry, I took care of it."

"You did what?"

"Do I get extra for neutralizing the trap?" Tobias asked.

The sage flipped the clasps on either side of the slender box and pushed the lid open. Peering inside, he examined the round dome of metal sitting inside, and growled in displeasure. "You idiot! This half-sphere is depleted. It's useless now!"

"If you want, I'll rehex it," Tobias said, hoping to remedy the situation.

"It doesn't work that way. Magic energy and radiation are non-compatible. While one can be used to neutralize the other, that is the extent of the relationship. Mutual annihilation, from which there can be no replenishment. What you have done is irreversible."

"How could I have known that?" Tobias asked defensively.

"You couldn't, and that is why I instructed you to leave the box shut!" The sage picked up the opened box and flung it across the room. The dome-shaped hunk of metal that had sat inside fell out halfway across the expanse, but both objects continued on their path, eventually hitting the side of the cave wall.

Shaking his head and staring at the odd objects on the table, the sage said, "You do realize what you've done, don't you? Without the proper fuel, I cannot complete the device."

Tobias couldn't believe it; refused to believe it. "No, you're just saying that."

The sage gave a peculiar smile to the accusation. "Do I ever just say things?"

"I suppose not," Tobias said, his frustration turning to dread. If what the sage said were true, as he knew it must be, then all he had been working toward was lost. His hopes and dreams, his very future, was being snuffed out before his eyes yet again, and it was all his own fault.

The sage turned his eyes away from Tobias and stared at the green and gold plates in front of him. "All these months we have spent together, honing your talents, teaching you to transcend the limited teachings of your vaunted Guild, all for naught. You may now be able to perceive the subatomic bonds of existence, yet what do you really know? The power has not removed your youthful arrogance, only emboldened it. How disappointing."

Tobias slapped his hands upon the desk, drawing the old man's attention. "You have taught me much, but still you hide the true extent of your wisdom. You should have told me more about the poisonous metal, so I would have known to deliver it unchanged!"

"As I've said, there are things beyond your comprehension, things I cannot reveal. I thought you had come to accept that."

"Blind faith is for the weak," Tobias said. "Do you fault me for seeking answers?"

"No," the sage said, shaking his head. "I fault you for not trusting me."

Tobias flinched as the sad words slapped him in harsh rebuke.

"For so long, we have served in this partnership," the sage continued. "You have come far in your mental training, and worked toward our mutual ends; to improve this world. However, as we near the completion of our desired goal, you question my orders, and unwittingly destroy the most vital element of our entire plan. I'm afraid without that radioactive ore, the engine I've built shall never restore a single human life."

Tobias understood the depth of his failure, but couldn't accept it. There had to be a means of rectifying the situation. "Please, Sage, you must complete the device! Isn't there more of this special metal, anywhere?"

"Of course there's more metal, but it's unrefined, and the technology required to create viable, fissionable material won't exist for decades."

"If that's true, then where did that piece come from?" Tobias asked, jabbing a finger toward the wall where the box had been flung.

The sage made an amused sound and fought back a smile. "Elsewhere, I'm sure."

Tobias hated it when the sage did that; speaking in vague terms which would tell you everything if you already knew the answer, but otherwise revealed nothing. The mysterious old seer had a peculiar way about him, an unearthly talent for perceiving the world at large. That is why Tobias called him *Sage*, for the old man had never given his name, nor any official title.

During these past months of association with him, Tobias had seen the sage perform many great feats. He'd witnessed firsthand the man's unique ability to predict the future, and positively locate people and objects over great distances with precision accuracy. The man's skills were clearly mystical in nature, though his power was far in excess of anything the Guild possessed. It was frightening and exciting at the same time to think that someone could harness such power.

The sage froze in mid-motion, gripping one of the strange plates so tightly it cracked. Closing his eyes, he breathed a deep breath, and then shivered. "There is a possibility," he mentioned, after he broke free from his brief trance.

"Yes?" Tobias said eagerly.

"Ferguson," the sage replied. "He may know where to procure another hunk of the metal, or he'll know who does. Extract the information from him if you wish your wife to live again."

Tobias nodded, and marched away without a second thought. He was eager to serve, if it meant bringing him closer to the one thing he cared about in this life; the one thing that had been taken from him far too soon.

He could remember that fateful day which had destroyed his life forever. The day his wife had died.

Her name was Sarah Smith. It was an ordinary enough name, and her charm had been just as plain. There'd been nothing magical about her, nothing you'd suspect would catch the eye of a proficient Journeyman Warlock, but somehow fate had lured her to Tobias. After a few chance meetings, the two had formed an affinity for one another, and within a year they were happily married.

Then, tragedy struck.

Tobias remembered receiving the call. He'd been studying in his chambers, preparing for the final Master's Examinations, when his junior apprentice had sent him a quick summons through the ether. The shout was urgent, but Tobias had ignored it for several minutes, as he sought to perfect mental discipline. No extraneous distraction should deter a true Master from his work, and such a minor thing as a nagging apprentice was just the sort of trick his teachers might use, attempting to trip him up. So, he'd ignored it, condemning his wife to death.

Two minutes too late, Tobias replied to the summons, and found the body of his wife lying in the street outside his Fulton Street home. An errant wagon had run her down, crushing her chest and legs. The injuries had left her silent in her final moments, even as the apprentice had called for help. Yet none had come.

The severity of the wounds would have been nothing for Tobias to heal, had he been there in time. His devotion to the mystic arts had cost him the only thing that really mattered in life, and it took Sarah's death for him to truly understand it. Her death had haunted him every day since then.

Weeks of grief were accompanied by heavy drinking, and it was then that the sage had found him, and offered to resurrect his lost love, *for a price*. To build the machine capable of restoring her required special parts and resources, and it had been Tobias' job to procure them by any means necessary. Nearly a year of theft and slaughter had left the young warlock quite detached from his emotions, at least where they pertained to his fellow human beings. Sarah was the only thing that mattered. The others were just target practice.

Venturing out to capture the final piece of the puzzle, Tobias reflected upon his life, and smiled. How curious that he had lost his soul in the name of love. He delighted in the irony.

* * *

Henry Currant was a small, unassuming man with small ears and big eyes. He was fast on his feet, and equally quick with his words, so he always appeared nervous. It was simply the way he was. Although his mannerisms made him seem shaky, he was a top notch telegraph operator, and never missed a beat; at least, none that his assistant could ever catch.

It was early Saturday morning when a telegram came across the wires for Sheriff Doliber. As usual, Henry scrawled down the message with a charcoal pencil and left his assistant to man the office while he ran over to deliver the message in person.

The sheriff was usually up by sunrise, but there was no sign of him as Henry came to the door. Peering in through the side window, he saw no activity whatsoever, and feared something was amiss. He tested the door latch and found it unlocked, so he proceeded inside. He stepped into the still room, his hand reaching for the .32 caliber Derringer pistol he always carried in his vest pocket. It was a great comfort to know that the weapon had been specially 'enhanced' by the sheriff. The bullets were specially saturated with a dispelling agent that could penetrate most any form of magic, and with good cause. Anyone capable of dispatching a warlock would have to be most proficient in magic, and would no doubt require more than an ordinary hunk of lead to stop them. Therefore, Doliber had been clever to equip the most trusted men of the town with a means of stopping such a potential threat. Never mind that it went against the Guild's explicit rules. He'd been bending those since graduation.

Henry crept across the room, glancing back and forth at the shadows, seeking whatever might lurk in the darkness. When he reached the sheriff's desk, he encountered no one, and felt more relaxed as he made his way up the stairs.

The long hallway at the top of the stairs had several doors on either side of it. Most of them were open, which gave Henry a clear view of a reading room, a small dining area, and two empty bedrooms. The last door on the left was shut, inviting the telegraph operator to investigate. When he grabbed the knob, a burning sensation flowed up his arm forcing him to jump back.

As Henry stood and rubbed his aching hand, the door in front of him opened, and an unkempt Sheriff Doliber stepped out. "Oh, it's you, Henry," he said as he brushed his ragged hair with a steady hand.

"One hell of a security system you've got there, Sheriff," Henry replied jerking his hand around to minimize the pain.

"It does the job," Doliber replied. "What can I do for you?"

"Telegram just came across the wire," Henry said, digging the piece of paper from his pocket and handing it to the sheriff.

Doliber glanced at the note, and read it aloud. "*From Marshal Albert Kingsley, stop. Been tracking team of rustlers near Vegas Springs, stop. Suspect northerly push, require assistance to head them off, stop...*" He turned his eyes from the paper and crumpled the note in his hands. With an irritated growl, he tossed the note against the wall and stormed down the hall.

Racing to catch up, Henry asked, "What's the matter, Sheriff?"

"I have matters of global importance weighing down on me. I don't have time to chase a bunch of yahoos running through the desert."

"Isn't that your job?" Henry asked, following Doliber down the stairs.

"Yes," Doliber replied through gritted teeth. "But there's only so much I can do. I have to prioritize, and right now I'm in the middle of something that demands greater attention." He stopped at his desk and reached for the box of cigars sitting there. He hadn't smoked in two days, and was in need of that soothing aroma.

Henry stood quietly as Doliber settled into his chair and lit his cigar with a spark of magic. As the sheriff calmed down from the first few inhalations, the telegraph operator said, "Do you want me to reply to the Marshal, and inform him of your inability to assist?"

Doliber blew out a thick cloud of smoke and shook his head. "Sit down, Henry," he requested in a more pleasant voice.

Henry complied, and took the waiting chair beside the desk. It wasn't a comfortable seat, just a couple of pine boards pegged together, but it beat sitting on the floor.

"I'm sitting on a hornet's nest here, Henry," Doliber said, handing his guest a cigar from the box.

"Oh?" Henry said, accepting the sheriff's hospitality. With a savage chomp, he ripped open one end of the cigar, and as he put it to his mouth the other end sparked to life with the help of a little enchantment. It was a handy trick, one Henry often wished he could duplicate.

"You've heard about the incident with the Ferguson and Finney stage?" Doliber began.

"Bits here and there," Henry mumbled around the cigar. He had the thing deeper in his mouth than was normal, as he played around with it.

"Yes, well, it was a warlock's doing, of that I'm certain," Doliber said reluctantly. It was a hazardous thing to admit, and the implications were still troubling him. "Worse, I'm pretty sure it's someone from the Guild; a graduate of the academy, possibly even a certified Master."

"I see," Henry said, unable to grasp the full gravity of the situation. "So, this bandit, or whatever, is one of your lot?"

"I wish it weren't the case, though I can see no other explanation," Doliber said, tapping his cigar against the brass ashtray on his desk. He left the smoldering stick there, as he reflected upon the images in his mind.

He'd spent the last two days in deep meditation and sleep. The stolen pieces of the Guildmaster's thoughts were a lot to assimilate, but little by little they were falling into place. There were several telling emotions he had recovered. The Guildmaster had been understandably worried, but mixed with that concern was a strange sense of elation, or excitement. Learning of the stagecoach heist had lifted his spirits for some reason, and solving that mystery remained Doliber's top priority.

Why would the senior-most warlock this side of the Rocky Mountains be overjoyed by a disgraceful act from a fellow guild member? To think that a trained mystic could use their powers for such wanton destruction was unthinkable. It went against everything the Guild taught, and held a penalty of death from the secret society of spell-casters. Any member committing such heinous crimes would never see a courtroom. They'd be "disappeared" by their fellows, and the due process clause of the Constitution be damned. Such was the price of their power.

There was obviously more to this case than Doliber could fathom. There was so little to go on, and he wasn't going to find the answers sitting around his office, or chasing common thieves. He needed a little more time to unravel the secrets trapped in his mind, and extraneous stimuli would only serve to hinder his efforts.

Still, he had a job to do, and there was no getting around it.

"So, what should I tell the Marshal?" Henry finally asked, after Doliber had filled him in about his current investigations.

After thinking it over, Doliber came up with a solution. He should have seen it all along, but had been too distracted by his other problems. Standing up and straightening his shirt, he said, "You tell Marshal Kingsley he'll get his backup, though don't expect it to be all that big."

* * *

Ron and Joella were riding at a steady pace through the thinning pines. After a full day of riding, they were still in California, which amazed Ron, for he hadn't expected them to be this far from the arid Nevada town of Selwood, where he'd been abducted by this treacherous elf. Truly, she must have used some enchantment to transport them such a distance in a single day, or he'd been unconscious a lot longer than he'd suspected.

"Physical relocation is one of the few talents I have," Joella admitted when asked about the length of their journey, "but it's spotty. Some days, I can move a few miles with a thought, others I'm stuck on foot. Hauling you and these horses all the way over two hundred miles wiped me out. I doubt I'll regain enough mystic equilibrium to teleport anytime soon."

"So we're stuck doing things the natural way," Ron added.

"At least you've got a ride," Joella said, patting her brown steed. "Are you sure you want to go back to Selwood? From what you've told me, the sheriff was trying to keep you like Mactus wanted me."

"Not quite," Ron said, seeing some parallels, but far different motivations. "He gave me his word I could decline his offer after I thought about it. Well, I've thought about it, and I say no. Soon as I pick up my pistol that you left with that snotty elvish barkeep, I'll be heading someplace else."

"Any idea where?" Joella asked, right before a tree branch smacked her in the face. She wiped a hand over her eyes and spit out a few needles.

Ron laughed. "That'll teach you to get distracted."

"At least I'm tall enough to catch a branch," Joella quipped. "You'd have to run into a tree head-on before anything hit you."

"Yep, being small has its advantages," Ron said, turning her obvious insult around. He recognized her antagonism wasn't malicious, and let it roll off his back.

As the mid-morning sun crept upwards, the foliage began to thin, and the ground grew sandy. They were reaching the dividing point between forest and desert, Ron suspected. They couldn't be too far from Nevada now.

A few more hours of riding brought them to a grassy meadow surrounded by scrub brush. There, they stopped to give the horses a rest and refill their canteens from a trickling brook. Joella knew this trail well, and the desert was fast approaching. Soon, their trip would be determined by the handful of springs hidden amongst the barren hills and plains. Over a hundred miles of sparse vegetation and arid sand awaited them on the trip back to Selwood, assuming they could take a direct route, but under full sunlight they'd need to rest frequently. Without pushing the horses, their trip could take a few more days.

While he sat and nibbled on some hardtack, Ron spotted a glint of light in the distance. Atop one of the hills a few miles away, a spark of light caught his eye for a moment. Following that flash, he thought he saw a humanoid figure there, though the distance was too great for him to be certain. He kept his view on that general area as he ate, seeing if his eyes were playing tricks on him, but it soon became obvious he was right. Someone *was* there, and getting closer.

When Joella came back from a short visit to the bushes, Ron pointed out the approaching figure. Grabbing a pair of binoculars packed in her saddlebag, she took a closer look, and positively identified it as a pale man with black hair, dressed in brown leather attire with a star pinned to his vest.

The brief description told Ron all he needed to know.

Twenty minutes later, Sheriff Doliber came walking up to the watering hole, looking calm and relaxed, as always. He was lacking a hat, which was something unheard of for men on the frontier, though there were many things unusual about this law man.

"What brings you out all this way, Sheriff?" Ron asked with a mouthful of dried meat stuck in his cheek.

"I've spent the last three hours trying to find you," Doliber replied coldly. "I thought we agreed you'd stay in town for a while."

"I didn't exactly go of my own accord," Ron replied, standing up. His height reached the sheriff's chest, so he was still looking up at the man as their conversation continued.

"Yes, well, we can settle that later," Doliber said, reaching for a piece of paper in his pocket. "I've got a job for you."

"Not interested," Ron said instantly.

Doliber ignored his protest and continued. "It seems a pack of rustlers out of Arizona is riding our way. Marshal Kingsley is in pursuit, but he needs back-up, and I'm currently indisposed with another case. I figure this would be a good job for you to cut your teeth on."

"What did I just say?" Ron asked, tired of the sheriff's selective hearing.

"You said you weren't interested," Doliber replied with a hint of irritation, "which is fine. Jobs aren't always interesting, but we have to do them, nonetheless."

Ron sighed and walked over to his horse. He knew he couldn't get out of this, but had to try. "You're out of your jurisdiction, Sheriff," he mentioned. "It's not even Nevada, let alone Nye County."

"As a bonded deputy, you are under my jurisdiction, even when traveling abroad," Doliber stated.

"We fought a war over slavery," Ron growled. "Last I checked, it was abolished. I ain't bonded to nothing, and you can't force me to fight."

"Why are you being so obstinate?" Doliber asked.

"Why can't you just leave a man alone?"

"I can't afford to let you go," Doliber replied. "Not right now. Trust me when I say there are things happening which could have dire consequences for this great nation, and the entire world."

"And this relates to me how?"

"As a duly elected law enforcement officer, I must see to my duties of maintaining order and justice in this arid wilderness, but I can't do it all. Right now, I need you—yes, you specifically—to help me. I helped you not so long ago. Now, can I count on you to help me?"

Ron thought on it a moment, and considered what was being asked of him. Was it truly that outrageous? The sheriff was correct in his presumption of debt. Without Doliber's help, Ron would never have succeeded in bringing his brother's killer to justice. The present request was only fair turnaround.

"Okay, I'll do it," Ron said, "but after this one, we're even. If I don't want to carry on as your deputy, you'll let me go, agreed?"

"If I must," Doliber said, sounding less than enthused. "Now, I have a lock on the Marshal's general position, so I can send you to meet him immediately."

Doliber raised his hand in a preparation to cast the spell, but before he could, Ron halted him. "I don't even have my gun," the dwarf said.

"Oh, I took the liberty of retrieving it from Solen at the saloon," Doliber said, pulling the revolver and its ammunition belt out of his jacket pocket. The bulk of the object was far in excess of what you'd expect to fit inside that little slot, yet it had fit, and without even leaving a noticeable mark on the outside of the overcoat. Yet another one of the sheriff's mystic tricks, no doubt. "You really shouldn't leave something this important lying around."

"Yeah, thanks for the advice," Ron said, grabbing the trusty pistol and hooking the belt around his waist. It felt good to have his weapon of choice again, like being reunited with an old friend.

"Ready?" Doliber asked, eager to get him to Marshal Kingsley.

Ron put up his hand and turned toward his horse. Mounting the steed with an ungallant leap, he positioned himself for a ride. "Ready."

Doliber raised his hand again, prepared to activate his magic teleport.

"Wait," Joella interrupted sharply, causing Doliber to cringe. "That's my horse."

"Shoulda thought of that before you married me," Ron rebutted. He wasn't sure who was a preferable master, the sheriff or his new wife.

"Married?" Doliber said with clear amazement. "I'm sure that's one hell of a story, but it'll have to wait. You have some rustlers to apprehend." The warlock sheriff raised his hand for a third time to cast his spell.

"Stop!" Joella snapped. Walking up to the sheriff, she asked, "Say, Sheriff, how much does a deputy get paid in your county?"

"Depends on the workload," he replied. "But I can promise Ron will get ten dollars a head for the rustlers, dead or alive. Does that satisfy you, Missus Grimes?"

"Sure, if you give me a badge and the same rate," Joella replied.

Doliber looked at her as if she were joking. "Excuse me?"

"You want help. I'm volunteering. Deputize me."

"You're a lady," Doliber said incredulously. "You can't honestly think I'd send you up against armed men."

"It's either that, or you leave Ron Grimes here with me," Joella said, poking a finger in Doliber's chest most rudely. "And before you think about snatching him away against my consent, you should know we're bonded by a proximity tether. If we're separated by any significant distance, he'll be paralyzed."

Doliber wasn't pleased, and wondered if it was worth putting up a fight. Dispelling an elvish tether would be a tricky thing, and it would cause further delay. Every minute they waited, Marshal Kingsley was without backup, and that could prove deadly. This had to be resolved quickly, and there was only one obvious solution.

"Why are we even arguing this?" Ron asked. "Let's go!"

"Fine, I'll send the both of you," Doliber said, turning to Ron, "but it'll be on your head if anything happens to her." Raising his hand for the teleport, Doliber finally cast the spell, enveloping

Ron, Joella, and both horses in a shimmering light that faded within seconds, sending them on their way.

* * *

The blinding light faded from Ron's eyes, and he became aware of his new surroundings. A rock outcropping was staring him right in the face, not ten inches from his horse's nose. Turning the steed around, he saw they were in a small canyon filled with rock and dusty soil. It could have been any number of places in southern Nevada, and the dwarf didn't know the region well enough to venture a guess.

Joella wasn't in plain sight, leaving Ron to wonder where she'd gone. She had to be nearby, for if she weren't that pesky tether of hers would be kicking in by now, leaving Ron as a limp sack of flesh. The teleport must have separated them somehow, but not by too much.

Directing the horse forward, Ron felt a lump in the seat of his pants. Reaching back, he pulled a folded hunk of paper out of his back pocket. Opening one of the many leafs, he could see it was a map. There were some pencil and pen marks over the lithograph, highlighting his position and nearby landmarks.

"Nice one, Sheriff," Ron mumbled as he refolded the map and tucked it away.

As Ron slid the paper into a front pocket on his vest, a gunshot spooked his horse. The steed lurched up and began to run, but Ron managed to stay seated, and fought against the charge. As another shot ricocheted on the cliff behind him, Ron managed to pull the horse to a stop and draw his pistol. Somebody was gunning for him, and he had to assume it was the rustlers he'd been sent to capture.

Hopping off the horse, Ron sidled up to the canyon wall, looking around. Those shots were likely coming from overhead, based on their trajectories. There were plenty of places up there for men to be perched, but none he could spot from his current vantage point. He had to move further into the open.

The horse helped to provide cover as Ron moved forward. The animal threatened to bolt with each gunshot, but his tight grip on the reins and reassuring whispers kept it from total panic. After a few steps forward, Ron grew convinced that the shots were not aimed at him, for his horse was too big a target to miss. That gave him some reassurance that he retained the element of surprise.

The canyon opened up as it curved, and Ron spotted two men hiding behind a sizeable boulder, being shot at from above. The shots were ricocheting against the stone walls, which explained the bullets that had made their way toward Ron.

One of the men behind the boulder stood up and fired a rifle, picking off one of the opposing men. A bearded man up on the canyon's edge keeled forward and dropped thirty feet onto a pile of rubble, twitching his last on the rock pile.

The man who'd stood up to take the shot received two bullets for his trouble. As the wounded man stumbled backwards and slid behind the boulder again, Ron spotted the silver shield pinned over his heart. That man had to be Marshal Kingsley.

Knowing whose side he was on, Ron took aim with his Remington and shot back at the men above the canyon. His aim was accurate, but the distance was far, and an uphill shot caused him to misjudge the target. His first bullet skirted the ground under the rifleman's feet, causing him to jump back out of sight.

The firing ceased for the moment, so Ron made a run for it, reaching the sheltering boulder without incident. There, he found a young man with a clean shave rushing to reload his nickel plated revolver, while the bearded Marshal bled silently.

Ron bent down to inspect the Marshal's wounds, and saw they were mortal. The man's breathing had already stopped.

Kneeling with his back to the wall, he heard a slight commotion from behind, and turned just as a pair of armed men came out of a cleft in the rock. By the time he turned around, it was too late, and they had him dead to rights. "Drop it," one of them said. He was a tall man with a brown mustache and a blued Colt in his smooth hand.

Ron set his revolver down slowly and gently, making sure not to make any sudden moves that might spook the gunman. Once he was unarmed, he raised his hands over his head and waited for his captor to make his next move.

"My name's Wyatt Earp. Who the hell are you?"

"I'm Boron Grimes, Deputy to Sheriff Doliber of Nye County," Ron replied.

"Last I checked, we were still in Clark County," Wyatt said, keeping his revolver pointed at the dwarf. "What are you doing down here?"

"Marshal Kingsley asked for help, so Doliber sent me."

"I believe him, Wyatt," the young man sitting behind the boulder said. "He took a shot at 'em, right after Kingsley was hit, helped scare 'em off."

Wyatt stood still for a moment, then raised his pistol. "Well, if Warren believes you, that's good enough for me. Nice to have you along, Deputy."

Ron reached out and shook Wyatt's hand, which felt smooth to the touch. The man hadn't seen much hard labor lately. "Pleasure to make your acquaintance. You ride with Marshal Kingsley long?"

"Not at all," Wyatt replied. "We just met up this morning. Turns out we were tailing the same pack of outlaws and ended up in the thick of it together." Pointing to the young man by the boulder, he said, "That's my little brother Warren over there."

Ron tipped his hat to the young man, and Warren did likewise.

"And this is Texas Jack Vermillion," Wyatt said, hooking a thumb over his shoulder.

Texas Jack was a slim man with bushy, black eyebrows and a bulbous nose. There was a perpetual scowl on his face, which may have been due to his current circumstances, though you never could tell. Many gunfighters out west were of the sour type, unwilling to lift their cheeks in the mildest levity.

As the men were getting comfortable with each other, a commotion arose from up the canyon, drawing everyone to the cover of the boulder. The sound of horses was quickly evident and they waited with pistols drawn, anticipating an approaching foe. Their guards diminished as the new arrivals came into sight.

Ron recognized the first rider immediately. It was Joella, looking a little shaken but none the worse for wear. Behind her, riding atop a grayish mare, was an emaciated man with reddened eyes and a shotgun aimed at her back. He smiled from behind an imperial beard and week-old stubble on his cheeks.

"Hey, Wyatt, look what I dug out of the rocks," the scrawny man shouted boisterously with a southern drawl.

"Damn it, Doc, shut up and get down," Wyatt growled back in a half-hushed tone.

"Aw, it's all clear now," Doc Holliday replied, bringing his horse to a stop beside the dead rustler. He glared down at the corpse on the rocks with his sinister eyes. "Who shot this one?" he asked.

"Kingsley did," Ron said, getting a dirty look from the emaciated man on horseback. Warren nodded confirmation which did nothing to relax Doc's expression.

Doc climbed down from the horse and tucking the shotgun under his left arm he drew his pistol with his right. With rapid ease, he fired the gun at the bloody body, adding an extra hole to its head.

"What did you do that for?" Joella asked.

"Never can be too sure," Doc replied, holstering his sidearm before going into a coughing fit. He clung to the reins of his horse for support until it passed.

"You don't sound so good," Joella mentioned.

Doc raised his shotgun again, and directed her to dismount. He moved both horses forward until they reached the men by the boulder. He jabbed Joella in the back with his shotgun and smiled at his friends.

"There's no need of that, Doc," Wyatt said sternly. "They're on our side."

"Like I said, you never can be too sure," Doc replied.

Joella walked over to Ron and wedged up against him in a reassuring manner. "Husband," she said so all of the strange men could hear. "Thank God you are all right."

"Well, ain't that peculiar," Texas Jack mentioned with a bitter connotation. "What's a deputy doin' bringin' his woman along on a ride?"

Doc Holliday cleared his throat and added, "Perhaps we could continue this conversation on the move, before those rustlers get too far ahead."

His friends agreed, and Ron posed no objection. The rustlers were on the run, and if they wanted to catch them they had to pursue. Sitting around in this canyon did no good, and only invited another ambush.

"Did you manage to find the other horses, Holliday?" Texas Jack asked.

"All but one of them," Doc replied as they started walking. "They're just up ahead. Figure Pete Spence must have gotten yours."

"Damn it, Doc," Wyatt interrupted. "We're not tailing Pete Spence."

"Coulda fooled me," Doc replied, climbing onto his horse. The walking was clearly too much for him.

"We all know Spence is hiding in one of Behan's cells right now," Wyatt reminded him.

"We'll see about that soon enough," Doc replied dubiously. Spotting the limp body by the boulder, he mentioned, "Well, Jack, I guess you'll have to use Kingsley's horse. Doesn't appear he'll be needing it anymore."

The path out of the canyon was narrow and rough, and by the time they retrieved the horses in a side channel and reached open ground, there was no sign of their enemies. The scraggly trees and the surrounding hills prevented a long view, though there were plenty of tracks. Half a dozen horses were on the move northwest, and that was their path to follow.

Episode Five:
The Vendetta Ride

April nights were cold in Clark County, but the Earp party decided against a large fire. There was no telling how far they really were from their quarry, and smoke had the nasty habit of traveling on the breeze. They built their fire in a small depression nestled beside a steep hill, which provided the most cover they could find, and they kept it to a minimum, just enough to warm their beans.

The location was ideal, for there was also an active spring nearby. Water was life in the arid land, and without it a man and his horse weren't long for this world.

After building a fire and refilling canteens, the posse sat down for an evening's rest. The Earp party was growing acquainted with Deputy Grimes and his unlikely bride, and they all seemed to be getting on very well, with the exception of Doc Holliday, who refused to hang around and socialize. "Think I'd better tend the horses," he said, walking off and leaving his friends to babysit the new arrivals.

"What I wouldn't give for a good steak about now," Warren mentioned, rubbing his arms together.

"Here," Ron said, digging a hunk of jerky out of his saddle bags. He ripped off a fair-sized hunk and tossed it at the young man.

Grabbing the hunk of dried meat, Warren attacked it with savage fury, ripping and tearing with his teeth as if he hadn't eaten in days. Texas Jack leaned over and tried to snatch a piece, and nearly had his hand bitten in the process.

"Mind carving me off a hunk of that?" Jack asked after recoiling from the ravenous Warren.

Ron complied, and threw another piece of meat across the fire. Jack grabbed it and stuffed the whole thing in his mouth, munching with equal vigor as the young Earp.

Ron looked up and saw Wyatt standing over him, glaring with narrowed eyes. There was anger in him, though over what the dwarf couldn't fathom.

"Stay here," Wyatt told everyone, and then left the sheltered campsite. He headed around the side of the hill, keeping his eyes peeled for any figures lurking in the night. After getting a fair distance from camp, he saw a figure sitting beneath a dead tree. A brief coughing fit from the shaded individual positively identified him.

"How are you holding up, Doc?" Wyatt asked on approach.

"As fine as ever," Doc Holliday replied, breathing as deeply as possible, his chest wheezing. "Are you alone?"

"Near as I can tell," Wyatt replied, certain he had not been followed. "They're getting worse," he said, then related the last scene from camp.

"Can't let them have meat," Doc said, shoving a hand into his jacket to retrieve a flask. "It'll hasten the process."

"It was hard to avoid," Wyatt defended. "The dwarf gave it to them."

Doc Holliday made a disparaging sound and took a swig from his flask.

"We're going to have to tell them," Wyatt said calmly.

After taking a second nip from his flask, Doc asked, "Why should we do that?"

"Jack and Warren are getting worse every night, and we don't know how long it'll take us to catch these bastards. If we don't tell the dwarf and his elf what's going on, it could cause trouble."

"What makes you think they'll understand?"

"I see it two ways," Wyatt answered. "Either we can trust them and be honest, or we can put a bullet in Warren and Jack here and now, and I'll be damned if I'll do that."

Doc coughed a few times as he began his response. "I believe you're missing the third and easiest option here."

Wyatt waited patiently for him to provide it.

"We put a bullet in the dwarf and the elf, then continue on without worry."

"That's not an option," Wyatt said, spitting out the words with a violent growl. "After what scum like these rustlers have done to us, how can you even talk about killing an honest law man?"

"We do not know his character, so it's presumptuous of you to call him honest," Holliday said, tucking his flask away. "Now, if it were just a dwarf we were dealing with here, I would consider giving him the benefit of the doubt, but we all know how underhanded the elves can be."

Wyatt shook his head.

"We both know what low regard elves have for those in Warren and Jack's position. They would gladly see them dead, rather than cured."

"We don't know if Joella is of that persuasion. There are lots of different elves, with many different values. You're just bitter about Big Ears Kate leaving you."

"Do not bring that howah into this!" Holliday snapped, stomping his foot. "This has nothing to do with her. You know I'm right. We'd be better off without those two tagging along."

"Perhaps," Wyatt said, turning to head back to camp. "But would it be right?"

"You picked a fine time to find your conscience," Holliday replied.

"What about yours?" Wyatt asked as he walked away.

"I'm afraid I coughed mine out years ago," Holliday replied, moving to follow.

Wyatt had no trouble finding his way back to camp. The moon was more than half-full now, and there wasn't a cloud in sight. This crisp spring evening, he found his mind sliding back to a simpler time, to those same cool nights of his childhood in Iowa. Shaded by darkness, he could imagine these barren desert hills were those fallow fields waiting for the plow, and his brother Morgan was back in bed, waiting to help with the planting. So much he'd lost, all because of a vaunted sense of duty, coupled with monetary ambition.

He now wondered if it wouldn't have been better to stay a farmer, though it was too late for that. The die had been cast. He and his family would now have to accept the consequences of their actions.

When he returned to camp, Wyatt found Jack and Warren tucked in their bedrolls, sleeping off the savagery that he knew coursed through their veins. It was going to be another rough night for them, and it would keep getting rougher until they caught those responsible for their current condition.

The dwarf and his elvish bride were still sitting by the fire, talking quietly, though as soon as they spotted Wyatt they grew silent. He wondered what they'd been saying about him, and what secrets they could be hiding. They were certainly not the most ordinary pair. What kind of deputy brings his wife along on a ride, anyway? She had some cockamamie story about being deputized, too, but what sheriff would do that to any woman?

Yes, these two were strange. Perhaps that would help with the explanations.

"Dwarf, come with me," Wyatt said at the edge of the firelight.

"The name is Boron Grimes," the dwarf replied, standing up. "What's this all about?"

"We need to talk, alone," Wyatt replied, giving the elf a scrutinizing gaze. Holliday was right about the pointies, and he couldn't be sure how she'd react to the truth. It made more sense to take the dwarf aside first and gauge his reaction.

Wyatt turned to leave the camp, and Ron followed him into the darkness. As the men left the sight of the camp, they bumped into Doc Holliday, who decided to accompany them on their midnight stroll.

Once they were a sufficient distance from camp to avoid being overheard, Wyatt started the conversation. "What do you know about werewolves?" he asked, being direct.

"Just what I read in the newspapers," Ron replied. "Why?"

Doc Holliday growled at Wyatt, then threw up his arms in resignation, showing his disapproval of what was about to be revealed.

"These rustlers we're chasing," Wyatt started, "at least one of them is a werewolf. Maybe more than one."

It was a startling revelation, but Ron was careful to keep his cool. He was never one to show fear, even if the prospect of chasing contagious creatures of the night scared the hell out of him.

"Did Marshal Kingsley know?" Ron asked, putting on his bravest front in light of the new facts.

"No," Wyatt replied. "We only met him in the thick of it, and didn't have time to explain."

It made sense, and explained a few things, such as why Doc Holliday would shoot a dead man in the head, *just to make sure*. Werewolves weren't easily killed, and lead bullets would only give the illusion of death. There was only one thing that could put one down for good: silver.

The plague of lycanthropy wasn't a new thing, though it had been all but eradicated in Europe during medieval times. However, the disease lingered in the Americas, and many native tribes did not see it as a disease at all, but as a blessing. Of course, it didn't affect them as it did the Europeans. There was nothing more dangerous than an Indian werewolf, as they remained fully lucid and in control of their faculties, even as white men became unthinking animals in the same state.

It had only been recently that the disease of lycanthropy had become a problem in the west. Even among the Indians, it had been a rare gift, one they didn't want to share, until they realized the white man couldn't harness the power of the plague. Once that revelation became widespread across the frontier, they began using it as a weapon, inflicting settlers with seemingly superficial bites whenever the opportunity arose.

There was a growing problem with werewolves as a result, though it was still a rare affliction. Besides for special order military contracts, factory ammunition with silver bullets was virtually unheard of.

"They say Custer's face was eaten off at the Little Big Horn," Ron recalled, fighting to maintain his rugged façade.

"They were outnumbered and ill equipped to deal with their enemy," Wyatt said. "We're not so outnumbered, and we've made some effective ammunition. With any luck, we'll put these rustlers down for good, before they can poison anyone else."

"Got any silver .44 caliber balls?" Ron asked, tapping the revolver at his side.

"Have you got a mold?" Wyatt asked.

"Of course," Ron replied.

"Then we'll melt a few dollars and get you some balls."

"Don't suppose he's got his own change, do you?" Holliday asked. "Money doesn't grow on trees."

"You might ask Joella," Ron suggested. "I'm pretty tapped out."

Wyatt looked over at Holliday and both men exchanged questioning looks.

"I would not recommend that," Holliday said after an awkward silence.

"Why?" Ron asked, perplexed.

Holliday stepped up to Ron, so both men could see each other plainly in the faint moonlight. "How much do you really know about elves?"

It was a simple enough question, and Ron was prepared to give a quick retort about how much everyone knew in regard to the pointy-eared devils and their uncouth ways. Though, this wasn't a time for flippancy, nor for offhand boasts. This was serious, and giving the question serious thought, Ron realized he didn't know all that much about elves. They were an ancient and mysterious culture who largely kept to themselves, and few outsiders bothered to learn their ways.

For a moment, Ron felt ashamed of his ignorance in the matter, though he soon dismissed it as an unavoidable result of his upbringing.

"A lot of elves do not look kindly on lycanthropes," Doc Holliday explained. "Their old world superstitions paint werewolves as the leper, incurable and damned by God. They do not accept the fact that it is a disease; rather, they paint it as a sign of divine punishment. They'll kill anyone who is infected, without a second thought."

"So?" Ron asked, seeing no problem with eradicating criminal rustlers for the greater good. It wasn't like they were innocent women and children minding their own business. These were diseased vermin who needed to be put down.

Wyatt gave Holliday another look, and after a coughing fit the sick doctor just shrugged.

"There's one other thing you should know," Wyatt said, sounding reluctant. "Today wasn't the first time we tackled with these rustlers. Truth is, they first hit us down in New Mexico, which is why we're here now."

"I figured there was some reason you'd come all this way. What'd they do, kill some of your posse?"

"Not exactly," Wyatt continued. "We were at the train station in Albuquerque, on our way to Colorado, when these bastards ambushed us. One of them bit Warren and Jack, almost took a bite out of me before we chased them off. We pursued them clear across Arizona afterwards, and here we are, still at it."

The picture was getting painfully clear for Ron as he pieced the facts together. A single bite from a werewolf was all it took to infect someone, and then you were cursed for life. To become a slave of that mystic plague was a fate no honorable man could wish on his worst enemy.

"You understand why we can't have your wife killing every lycanthropic victim," Wyatt concluded.

"But what other option is there?" Ron asked. "If I had a choice between being a werewolf and being dead, I'd take a bullet any day."

"There is an alternative," Holliday interjected. "I believe there is a cure for lycanthropy. It has not been widely pursued by modern scientists or mystics because the plague was nearly extinguished centuries ago. Though, as you know, modern times are seeing a resurgence of it. Therefore, the old treatments are being revisited by some healers outside of the mainstream, you understand."

Hearing him speak of a cure, Ron wondered if Sheriff Doliber wouldn't be of help. The sheriff was a journeyman warlock of impressive skill, with connections to an esteemed guild of sophisticated wizards. If there were a cure, he'd probably know it, or know where to find it. "If you're looking for a cure, I may know someone who can lead you to it." Ron said.

Doc Holliday grunted. "I've already got the cure. I merely need the source of the infection before I can concoct an antidote."

"You?" Ron asked. Based on the man's gruff demeanor, he'd assumed the title "Doc" to be purely ceremonial.

"I was a learned man before the curse of tuberculosis deterred me from my chosen profession of dentistry. During my illness, I've sought out treatment with little success, but the journey has taught me a thing or two about other ailments and their cures. Unlike my own affliction, lycanthropy is treatable, but I must find the man who infected Warren and Jack to do so."

"Then we'll find him," Ron said, feeling bold. He was starting to get a taste for helping people, and the thought of ending the scourge of lycanthropy was appealing. There was a purpose to this pursuit, more than simply policing men. It was no longer a matter of justice, but of saving lives and bettering society as a whole. *That* he could understand, and appreciate.

"But, like I said," Doc added, "elves do not believe in curing lycanthropy. That's why we can't tell your wife about this."

Ron could see his point, but wondered if it were valid. Joella wasn't your typical elf, and though Ron didn't know her all that well, he had the feeling she'd be more open to possibilities. He'd lived this long by relying on his gut, though his instincts also told him not to argue with these men.

"What should we tell her?" Ron asked. "We can't leave her completely in the dark."

"We'll tell her what she needs to know," Wyatt interjected before Holliday could reply. "We'll tell her these bandits we're chasing are infected, and we've got to stop them before they hurt anyone else."

"Agreed," Ron said, feeling it would suffice. So long as she knew what they were up against, she'd be all right. They could worry about the rest of it later.

"Now that we've cleared the air, I think it's about time we got back to camp," Wyatt said. "We've got a long day ahead of us tomorrow."

* * *

They were on the trail before dawn, saddling up as the faint glimmer on the horizon vanquished the twinkling stars. They'd have to be swift if they wished to catch the pack of rustlers and find the werewolf among them.

The trail was easy to follow, almost as if their quarry wanted to be chased. Though, it was more likely a sign of desperation. These rustlers knew they were being tailed, and after weeks of hard riding they'd failed to shake their pursuers. By now, it was obvious their hunters would not stop until they were caught, and if they were caught, they'd be dead soon thereafter. Yesterday's shootout had proven that.

Wyatt looked over at the dwarf riding beside him, and wondered how the little man would feel if he knew the full story behind this ride. He hoped not to find out.

The cool of the night quickly vanished with the rising sun, which caused them to slow their pace and give their horses rest. It wasn't convenient, but it was necessary in the heat.

The rolling hills soon flattened out, giving them a good view of the terrain up ahead. There were still dips and canyons that could conceal the rustlers, though there was only so long they could hide. The Earp party was determined to catch up, and nothing could deter them.

At mid-morning they slowed down as the trail got vague. Several different riders had come through these parts recently, so they had to do some figuring, and pick a set of tracks to follow. Jack was a decent guide, and Joella offered to accompany him as he rode ahead to assess the situation. They were half a mile across a rocky plain before any word was spoken.

"There," Jack said, pointing to a few deep hoof prints dug into hard clay. "See them markings? Unshod ponies. Most likely Indian tracks, not our guys."

"The other set was heading north," Joella mentioned.

"Yep," Jack replied, "so unless we're way off, that's them."

The two rode back at a steady pace, trying to keep their horses fresh for the next leg of the chase. As they neared their companions, Joella had the urge to satisfy a point of curiosity. "So, where are you from in Texas, Jack?" she asked, seeking to open up a polite dialog.

"I'm from Virginia," Jack replied, keeping his eyes on his friends up ahead.

"Oh," Joella said, feeling the brush-off, but unwilling to accept it. "Then why do they call you *Texas*?"

"It's a long story," Jack said. "Let's just say that some Yankees don't know the difference between one southern accent and another."

The last hundred yards of their ride was done in silence. Wyatt rode up to meet them as they returned, and Jack explained what he'd deduced.

"They must be headed for Vegas, hoping to bed down for the night," Joella remarked after Jack's explanation. "It's the only settlement within range, and Army presence is sporadic. I'm not sure who's stationed there at the moment."

"You seem to know a lot about these parts," Wyatt replied, rubbing dust out of his mustache.

"I've been all over this part of the country," Joella said, leaving out the reason for her past travels. Her late husband, Vincent Lafayette, had been an unscrupulous character, one who'd dragged her along on his early travels.

Joella cherished that first year of their marriage, for she'd actually felt wanted. Their relationship had seemed right then, even when she was sleeping on the ground or hanging back while Vincent rode off on some criminal venture. Theirs had been a real partnership for a time, though the honeymoon period hadn't lasted.

After a year of riding together, Vincent had had his fill of marital bliss, and he subsequently dumped his wife off at home, preferring to share a prostitute's bed when coming in off the trail. Joella had seen him less and less, and grew to hate the drunken scoundrel. By the time of his death, she'd been glad to see him go.

The marriage had made her strong in many ways, and the early traveling had given her a working knowledge of southern Nevada. That information was proving to be invaluable.

The pursuit continued across the land of dusty soil and sparse weeds. After a few miles, the tracks disappeared onto a well-ridden trail, which continued in a northerly direction, but Joella advised a detour. Having ridden this route before, she knew the main trail wasn't the shortest route to Vegas. It curved toward the west over a span of ten miles, adding significant distance. If they skipped the path and made a direct bee-line for Vegas, they could cut several of those miles off the journey and possibly catch up to the rustlers.

The ride was rough over rocky hills, but the horses handled it well. Within two hours, they were back on the road, and within sight of the Vegas outpost. They were at least a mile off, but so was the group of six men they spotted coming up the road behind them.

"Ready for it, boys?" Wyatt asked as he drew the revolver from his belt.

"As ever," Doc replied, taking a quick nip from his flask before drawing his own pistol.

The others followed suit, arming themselves for the coming confrontation. Ron and Joella stood ready, though their effective ammunition was in short supply. Six silver balls were all that Ron had been able to make from the spare change in Joella's pocket. Fortunately, Joella's revolver took the same .45 Schofield cartridges that Jack's current revolver used, so he'd been willing to share a few rounds, but only a few. There would be no reloading for them, so they'd have to make each shot count.

The rustlers abruptly stopped about a hundred yards away. Spotting the Earp party which stood in their way, the men quickly dismounted, clearly done with running. They set their horses in front of them, building a defensive wall of equine flesh.

"Good, we can finally get this over with," Jack said, clicking his revolver's cylinder to check that he was fully loaded.

"They have nowhere to run," Joella mentioned, suspecting these rustlers knew as little about this area as Wyatt's men did. Unless you knew where to look, it was hard to find water in the arid lands, and Vegas Springs was the only mapped source within short riding distance. Death by gunfire could be preferable to lethal dehydration.

Everyone on both sides held their fire, waiting for the other side to shoot first. Rifles and pistols glistened in the sunlight, cocked and at the ready. The range was far, but each man knew the art of killing well.

"What are they waiting for?" Warren asked, as he trained his rifle on one of their horses.

Seeking to end the stalemate, Wyatt shouted to the rustlers. "We're after Pete Spence," he said, giving Doc a dubious look. "Send him out, and you can ride on."

"Pete's not here," a deep voice replied.

Wyatt turned back to Doc. "I told you, Spence is locked up in Tombstone."

"No!" Doc growled. Standing up and raising his pistol, he shouted, "I'll prove he's here!"

Doc's first shot skirted the ground directly in front of the line of horses. The rustlers replied with a volley of bullets, most of which went astray, but a few sank into Joella's horse. The wounded animal lurched to the side as it tried to run away, but fell in the attempt. Joella was almost caught under its heavy mass, but managed to dart out of the way.

The Earp party responded in kind, sending bullets at the wall of horses. Two of the animals dropped quickly, but four more continued to provide cover for the rustlers. Warren got a clear shot with his rifle, and picked off one man's head as it poked up for a look, but the others were too shielded.

"We need to get closer," Jack shouted as ricocheting bullets kicked dirt onto his feet.

"Good luck with that," Doc said, firing again. His latest shot managed to hit one of the fallen horses, doing little good.

As the volleys of gunfire continued, Joella noticed Ron standing behind his horse, watching the exchange. "Why aren't you firing?" she asked as she took aim.

Ron didn't reply, but continued his quiet observance. He had yet to fire for very good reason; he was waiting for a clear shot. As the bullets burned through the air around him, he stared at the rustlers, saw their cover diminish as horse after horse collapsed. It wouldn't be long before he had his chance to end the conflict. Patience was the key. He was going to save his bullets for when they'd really count.

The rustlers weren't terribly accurate, but one finally had a lucky shot. Warren screamed in agony as a bullet sank into his shoulder, forcing him drop his rifle. Nobody had time to check on him, not in the thick of it.

The final of the rustlers' horses whinnied in protest after being hit, leaving the five standing men relatively exposed. That was what Ron had been waiting for, and he stepped forward to take aim with his Remington. He shot round after round, taking careful aim at his opponents. Wyatt joined him, while everyone else reloaded. One by one, the silver bullets found their targets, and when both men had emptied their cylinders, silence finally prevailed. The gunfight was over.

As the dust settled, Joella tended to Warren's wound while the other men marched forward to inspect the dead and dying rustlers.

They came upon the band of rustlers and studied their faces, looking for someone familiar. Doc rolled a man over with the toe of his boot, hoping to see Pete Spence, only to be disappointed. The man was unfamiliar, a total stranger.

"Damn it, Spence has to be here," Doc said after seeing the last of the rustlers.

A peculiar chuckle came from one of the wounded men who still clung on to life. Everyone turned to see the source of the laughter, an Indian leaning against his dead horse.

"Indian Charlie," Wyatt said, pointing his gun at the wounded man who continued to laugh, even though it clearly pained him.

"I told you, Pete's not here," Charlie said with amusement. The bullets in his chest would soon silence him, but he didn't seem to care.

"You look pretty happy for a dead man," Wyatt challenged, cocking his pistol. "I already killed you once. This time, I've got the right bullets to make it permanent."

"You murdered my friends, hunted us like dogs," Charlie said, growing bitter in his tone. "What sort of law is that?"

"You bastards killed my brother Morgan, and tried to kill me! Now you have the nerve to lecture about the law?"

Charlie paused a moment, and then replied. "I shall have my revenge. Your friends will never be free of the wolf-spirit. Death will be their only recourse."

"Not if I have anything to say about it," Doc said, digging around in his vest pocket. He removed a piece of linen and unfurled it, revealing a tiny sprig of wolfsbane. He waved it in front of Indian Charlie, and the wounded man cringed.

"Yep, as I thought," Doc said, waving the dried plant in front of Charlie again, just to watch him squirm. "Assuming you're the source, it should be easy to formulate an antidote for Warren and Jack."

Even the presence of the wolfsbane couldn't stop Charlie from laughing at Doc's assertion. Wyatt kicked the chuckling Indian and demanded an explanation.

"I am not the one who bit your friends," Charlie said. He coughed up a bit of blood and struggled to stay conscious.

"Who did?" Wyatt asked.

Charlie looked up and smiled, leaving the question unanswered.

"It was Pete Spence, wasn't it?" Doc said, stuffing the wolfsbane back in his pocket. "I knew I saw him in Albuquerque."

Charlie stopped smiling, clearly discontented at Doc's deduction.

"I don't get it," Jack interrupted, pausing from his looting of the bodies to join the conversation. "I thought Spence was in protective custody. What was he doing in New Mexico?"

"He came for revenge," Charlie answered, "to assure you would pay for your crimes. As Pete was the one to bite your friends, only his blood can serve your needs for a cure, and only until the next full moon completes their transformation."

"You son of a bitch," Wyatt said. Full of rage and adrenaline, he pulled the trigger at point-blank range, putting a silver bullet into Charlie's forehead. The Indian slumped down as the final breath passed his lips.

With the last of the rustlers dead, Wyatt put his gun away.

The answer was becoming clear, though nobody said it. This entire run had been a diversion, a way for Pete Spence and Indian Charlie to assure they'd get their revenge. All this time, Wyatt's party had been chasing the wrong men, taking them further and further away from the one man who held the key to a cure. It would take them days to get back to Tombstone, assuming that's where Pete Spence was hiding, and by then the moon would be in decline. It would be too late for Warren and Jack.

Doc grabbed a handkerchief out of his pocket and began sopping at the bloody wounds on Charlie's body. "I'll see what I can do," he said. "Maybe we'll get lucky."

* * *

The Earp party rode into Vegas Springs an hour after their bloody gunfight. As they approached, a dozen soldiers rode out to greet them. The authorities were ready for battle, understandably so, though Wyatt flashed his badge and gave them a brief explanation which allayed their concerns. Most of what he said was true, though he left out the personal motivations behind his actions. The commanding colonel let them proceed into town, though assigned two of his men to keep an eye on them.

Ron had a funny feeling about these alleged law men, as more of the truth sank in. None of this seemed terribly lawful, their pursuit of the rustlers or the execution of Indian Charlie. It was clear that Wyatt had sought vengeance, rather than justice. Ron could relate, having dispatched his brother's killer not so long ago, but that didn't mean he could trust any of his new acquaintances.

There wasn't much to Vegas; a dozen houses and the army barracks near the life-giving springs; little more than a way-station, and a depository of goods for a handful of ranchers in the surrounding area. It was hard to believe there was much farming going on in this part of the country, but Joella said the land was suitable for subsistence living in certain places. It was also plausible that amateur magicians made a living augmenting the poor soil and assuring adequate moisture for the crops. With the blessings of magic, any land could be inhabited.

It was mid-afternoon by the time they got settled at the local flop house. The place was drafty, but the beds were clean. Ron felt it was as good a time as any for a nap, so he left the others to their business and caught up on the sleep he'd lost over the past few nights.

The room wasn't much more than a hole in the wall. The bed took up most of the space, and it was hardly large enough for a full-grown man. Fortunately, Ron was smaller than your average lodger, so it suited him just fine. He shut the door and flopped down on the lumpy mattress, feeling ready to doze off in spite of the full daylight shining in through a small window. He'd learned to rest at odd hours over the years.

As Ron felt the curtains of slumber tugging at his consciousness, a hollow voice echoed around him. "Deputy Grimes, status report!"

It took him a minute to realize it was Sheriff Doliber's voice interrupting his rest.

"I was about to get some sleep. How's that for status?" Ron replied impertinently.

"I know," Doliber replied. "I've been watching you remotely for the last hour."

"Just an hour? I thought you'd be spying more often," Ron said, suspecting this outing to be a well-monitored test.

"I've been busy," Doliber's voice answered. "That's why I sent you in the first place, so I could attend to other matters. Now, what happened?"

Ron rolled over onto his side and felt a lump of cotton digging into his shoulder. "Can't this wait? I'd like to get some shut-eye."

The sheriff's voice disappeared, and Ron started to drift off to sleep. Before he could, the voice returned.

"I see," Doliber mentioned.

"See what?" Ron asked.

"Why you were reluctant to explain the situation," Doliber said with crystal clarity. His voice had suddenly lost its echo, and sounded much closer, unlike the remote tone it had been.

Ron opened his eyes and saw Doliber standing beside his bed, looking very imposing with his tanned leather outfit and exposed gun-belt. The startled dwarf rushed to attention, sitting up on the edge of the mattress.

"Oh, don't get up on my account," Doliber replied, turning to look out the tiny window at the foot of the bed. "By all means, get some sleep."

Ron grumbled to himself and stood up. The opportunity for rest had passed, as the sheriff's disturbance had snapped him awake. There was no way he'd be able to fall asleep now, not in broad daylight and a jolt of adrenaline coursing through his veins.

"So, what do you want to know?" Ron asked, wondering how much Doliber had deduced.

"Oh, I have what I need," Doliber replied, tapping his temple with two fingers. "I scanned your mind."

Ron frowned and stood up. "Ain't nothing off-limits to you magic meddlers?"

"I needed information, and you weren't being forthcoming." Doliber saw Ron shooting daggers with his eyes. "Don't worry, it was only a passive reading. Your deep, dark secrets are safe, other than those you did over the last day or so."

"I do a lot of thinking," Ron said, wondering how many questionable concepts flowed through him on a regular basis. He was a man, after all. So was Doliber, but that didn't mean he had the right to pry on another man's daydreams. Ron had no idea how much the sheriff had seen of his involuntary imaginings, but to think he'd seen any of them was unpleasant.

"Yes, I realize that," Doliber answered, looking thoughtful. "But a passive scan only reveals sensory memories, what you saw and heard... maybe a touch of emotion comes through. Now, can we get down to business?"

"What would that be?" Ron asked, being purposely obtuse.

"We have a pair of potential werewolves downstairs," Doliber reminded. "That could be a problem."

"Can't you take care of it? Spin a little magic remedy for what ails them?"

"I'm afraid not," Doliber replied. "There are a lot of diseases that magic has yet to cure; lycanthropy and consumption are among them."

"My Uncle Brizban was shot three times at Gettysburg, and the Medlocks patched him right up, even healed a shattered leg. How is it you can't conjure up a cure for these folks?"

"Knitting tissue and bone is a lot different than curing plague. There are still a lot of things we don't know about the human body, and I'm not a warlock of medicine at any rate. So, that leaves us with one option."

"And what's that?" Ron asked.

"We wait to see if Doc Holliday's miracle cure really works," Doliber replied.

* * *

Joella was alone in Miller's Restaurant, the downstairs portion of the boarding house. A dozen tables were crammed together into a cramped eating area, and a counter sat opposite the door. The small establishment doubled as a saloon, with a rack of whiskey bottles set against the back wall. There weren't any drovers or cowboys in town at the moment, so the place wasn't seeing much business.

The peace and quiet was nice after a day of hard riding and getting shot at. She'd just spent the past hour cleaning everyone's guns, which entailed pouring scalding water down the bores and pulling oiled patches through to remove black powder residue. If left uncleaned, the filth would corrode the metal.

A bell rattled as the door opened, and Wyatt came inside. Joella didn't pay him much attention as he sat down beside her, and simply nursed the glass of water she had in front of her.

The proprietor of the establishment, Erwin Miller, Jr., came slouching into the room after hearing the bell. The middle-aged man with prematurely-white hair didn't look terribly enthusiastic as he came over to see what his newest customer wanted.

"Coffee, black," Wyatt requested, slapping a nickel down on the counter.

"Big spender," Erwin mentioned with disdain, grabbing the five-cent piece and eyeing it suspiciously. A large 5 sat surrounded by thirteen stars on one side, and a striped shield occupied the other. He shook his head slightly and slid the coin into his pants pocket before leaving to fill the order.

"Where are your friends?" Joella asked.

"Doc's taking care of them," Wyatt replied. "I hope you don't think we're ungrateful for your help, but as soon as Warren's patched up, we'll be leaving on our own."

"Oh?" Joella asked politely.

"We were headed to Colorado before these rustlers got in our way. My brother James went ahead of us to secure accommodations, so we've got some time to make up."

"What's in Colorado?" Joella asked, getting nosy.

"Nothing in particular," Wyatt said, avoiding an explanation.

"Hoping to get some peace and quiet for a change?"

"Something like that," Wyatt said as Erwin returned with his coffee. He waited until the surly barkeeper was back in the kitchen before adding, "I reckon I've seen enough bloodshed for a while."

They sat and sipped their drinks for a minute, until Doc Holliday came bursting through the doors. The withered man collapsed on the floor, gasping for breath with congested lungs. Wyatt helped him up off the floor and set him in one of the nearby chairs.

"It was the wrong blood," Doc uttered between gasps and coughs.

"What's happened?" Wyatt asked, gripping Doc's shoulders to keep him from falling over.

After the coughing fit subsided, Doc answered. "They've succumbed to the infection."

Wyatt stepped back and brushed a hand over his hair in a shaky manner.

Joella downed the last of her water and joined the conversation. "What is he talking about?"

"I am so sorry, Wyatt. I never thought the wrong blood would have that effect," Doc said, starting to tear up.

Wyatt said nothing, but reached for his revolver. Joella thought he was going to pull it on Doc for a minute, but as the weapon was drawn, the law man turned for the door. Time became palatable as Joella watched him clomp to the exit and push his way outside. She had to see what was happening, and know what Wyatt would do next, so she pursued, leaving Doc Holliday alone to nip at his flask.

A woman's scream greeted Joella as she ventured out into the sunlight. She turned her head to see a pair of ladies racing along the side of the road, holding up their cumbersome dresses as a large silver-gray wolf sprinted after them. The beast had blood dripping from its teeth, revealing it had already tasted prey.

As the women ran by, Wyatt took aim and shot at the wolf. The bullet skimmed the top of the beast's shoulders, but that didn't slow it. The wolf zipped past, getting dangerously close to the women it pursued. In moments, a wicked curse would be spread to the women, assuming they survived the mauling.

Wyatt stiffened his stance and took careful aim, holding the revolver with both hands. Squeezing the trigger, his shot proved more accurate, sinking a bullet behind the werewolf's skull. The savage beast collapsed in mid-stride, as did one of the women who caught a piece of ricochet in her calf.

The werewolf twitched in the throws of death, and as the life faded from the creature, a metamorphosis occurred. In a matter of seconds, the hairy exterior and dog-like features vanished, replaced with the naked body of Texas Jack Vermillion.

Joella walked over to look upon the dead man, remembering him just an hour ago, and suddenly realizing the truth these men had been hiding from her. The true purpose of their mission was not one of justice or revenge. Dread filled her as it all sank in. "How could you keep this from me?" she shouted.

"We didn't know how you'd react," Wyatt explained as he came over. The gun was still in his hand. "Elves are known to kill werewolves on sight."

Joella turned around and tensed her arm, feeling the urge to punch someone. "Bigoted rumors spread by petty men!" she cursed. "I could have saved him!"

"You what?" Wyatt asked, maintaining a cold front.

"My clan has used magic and alchemy to exorcise lycanthropes for decades. If you'd told me the truth..." She trailed off, shaking her head in dismay.

"I can't believe that," Wyatt said. "I've known plenty of elves, and I've never heard of any cure!"

"You obviously knew the wrong elves. If you'd known anyone from Clan Talus..." Joella stopped as her eyes spotted a hairy figure slinking in the distance. She pointed over Wyatt's shoulder, and he turned to see what she'd spotted, a wounded werewolf staggering on three legs. It had to be Warren. The bullet hole through his shoulder had not healed with his lycanthropic transformation. As such, he was sluggish and disabled, a much easier target.

Wyatt raised his revolver, ready to fire.

"It's not too late. I can still save him!" Joella shouted.

Without a word, Wyatt pulled the trigger.

Joella closed her eyes as the shot went off, unwilling to see this law man kill his own brother. The very human scream that followed prompted her to open them again, and she saw a uniformed Army corporal staggering to the ground, dropped by Wyatt's bullet. A second round was fired from Wyatt's gun, and this time a young private screamed and gripped his shoulder, dropping his rifle on the boardwalk across from the boarding house.

With the soldiers out of the picture, Wyatt looked over his shoulder at Joella. "You'd better be telling the truth."

Joella nodded her response, and they both ran over to Warren the werewolf, who growled and snapped at them when they came near. His mind was totally suppressed, and every shred of humanity was gone. All that existed at that moment was this transformed animal which instinctually sought to spread its disease.

"All right, Mrs. Grimes, time to weave that elvish magic of yours," Wyatt said, keeping his revolver aimed at the wolf.

"That's Grimes-Talus," Joella corrected as she put out her opened hand. "Give me some silver. A coin, a bullet, anything!"

Wyatt reached his free hand down to his gun belt and pulled a cartridge out of a loop. He handed it to Joella without taking his eyes off the wolf that continued to growl and glare back at him.

Gripping the cartridge in her hand, Joella closed her eyes and began to hum. The calm and steady meditation allowed her to focus her limited mystic abilities, which she channeled into the silver bullet. A pale blue glow emanated from her hand, and she opened her eyes wide. The light burst from her hand and followed her gaze, striking the werewolf directly on the snout. In response, the beast leapt up on its hind legs and stared up at the sky, howling at the midday sun. The metamorphosis that followed occurred much like it had for Jack, quickly and completely, only this time it wasn't caused by death.

When it was all over, Warren stood there, stark naked, dazed and confused in the middle of the street. Glancing around, he spotted his brother right in front of him and asked, "Did it work?"

"What do you remember?" Wyatt asked, directing his brother to head for the boarding house.

Warren lowered his head, trying to think. "Last thing I recall, I was swallowing this dirty concoction Doc had mixed up. It burned my throat pretty bad. I must have blacked out after that."

A shot was fired, and a bullet sailed past Wyatt's field of vision, missing his nose by mere inches. He looked up and down the street, and spotted one of the soldiers he'd wounded crouched against a porch post, struggling to aim his pistol.

"We've got to get off the street," Joella said.

"We've got to get out of town," Wyatt replied, "before the colonel comes back and has us all hanged."

"Somebody mind explaining to me what's going on?" Warren asked, flinching as another bullet zinged by his head.

"Doc botched the cure," Wyatt said, as they reached the boarding house door. "I had to shoot Jack, and would've shot you if not for Joella here."

"I managed to arrest the symptoms," Joella explained as they walked into Miller's dining room. "For a lasting cure, we'll need to see the medic in Ravenna-West."

Doc Holliday was standing beside the door when they entered, and kept an eye on the street from his vantage point. "So, we've declared war on the Army now?" he asked condescendingly.

"It was that or let them kill my brother," Wyatt said. "It was self defense."

"I doubt they'll see it that way," Doc replied, watching the wounded private collapse half a block away. As the wounded soldier hit the ground, a shimmer of light surrounded him, and in seconds he was gone, spirited away in a flash of magic.

Doc cursed after seeing the display, fearing the worst. "Damn Army's got a 'lock in the ranks." He stuck his head out far enough to see where the corporal had fallen, but saw only an empty patch of street. Both men were gone!

Wyatt could tell his run was nearing an end. For all they had done—the miles they had ridden and the men they had killed—it was about to result in a prison cell, the last place a former law man wanted to be. It was a dreaded defeat, but there was one positive result from it all.

Gripping Warren's arm, Wyatt said, "There's no need for you to stick around. Go with the elf and that dwarf of hers. Get out of

Vegas, and keep riding until you're where you need to be for the full cure."

"The hell with that, Wyatt, I wanna fight!" Warren protested.

Wyatt shook his head. "We spent all this time hunting those rustlers down so you could live. I'm not going to have all our efforts wasted."

"Nor am I," Doliber's commanding voice said, snapping everyone to attention.

Sheriff Doliber came down the sturdy flight of stairs that led up to the bedrooms. Accompanying him were Deputy Grimes and the two soldiers Wyatt had shot. The enlisted men weren't injured in the least, though they didn't look very happy as they took a position in front of the bar.

Wyatt sized up the situation, and came to a likely conclusion. "So, you're going to bring me in, Sheriff?" he asked, spotting the star pinned to Doliber's chest. "It's okay; I'll go quietly, just leave my brother out of it."

"No," Doliber said.

"But Warren's got nothing to do with this. He didn't shoot those soldiers, I did."

"That's not what I mean," Doliber continued. "I understand what you were trying to do. Corporal Baines here was about to shoot your brother, so you did the only thing you could to stop him. If I'd been in your position, I might have done the same."

"So now what, the Army gets to hang me, instead?"

"You're free to go," Doliber said.

"But I shot those men," Wyatt said, seeming interested in condemning himself. The guilt of his vendetta ride was influencing his judgment, even if he didn't realize it.

"You may have shot at them, but I made sure the bullets didn't cause any real damage. Oh, I provided the illusion of injury, so I could gauge your true reaction, but I'm satisfied with the way you conducted yourself."

"That's it?" Wyatt asked, wary of Doliber's motivations. "What about them?"

"I've talked it over with the boys here," he said, hooking a thumb at the soldiers. "They'll cover for you, and so will I under one condition. Leave Nevada, and never come back."

"You don't even have to ask," Wyatt said, finally willing to accept the acquittal.

Their run was at an end, and Wyatt saw no reason to press his luck by sticking around a minute longer. With Doc Holliday and Warren in tow, he headed for the door, eager to kick up some dust and ride for the State line.

"Head for California," Joella advised as the men stepped outside. "When you reach Mono Lake, ask for directions to Talus County. You'll find what Warren needs there."

"Much obliged, ma'am," Wyatt said, tipping his hat in farewell.

As the Earp posse headed for the stables, the two soldiers stepped outside to watch them go. It was their assignment to keep track of the men while they were in town, and that's what they continued to do. Doliber and Ron went out to see to it that was all the soldiers did, and watched as Wyatt, Warren, and Doc trotted out of town.

"You're really gonna let 'em ride out?" Ron asked.

"Of course," Doliber replied. "This county's not my jurisdiction, and even if it were, I wouldn't feel inclined to arrest a man for defending his family."

"Even if that entails shooting soldiers and protecting a werewolf?"

"Obviously," Doliber said. "But I saved the soldiers, so no harm done."

"You're a good man, Sheriff. Maybe I'll stay on as a deputy for a while, after all," Ron said, finding the allure of the job outweighing his past reservations. He could make a real difference in this wild country, and get paid for it. The time had come for Ron to accept his fate.

"I'm glad you're finally coming around," Doliber said, looking down at the short man. There was satisfaction painted all over his face, which covered up the worry that lurked beneath the surface. The answers he'd been seeking in the stagecoach robbery were finally unraveling to his mind's eye, and that spelled trouble.

Episode Six:
The Villain Emergent

The damaged stage coach rolled into the loading yard behind the Ferguson and Finney building on the east side of Sacramento. After learning of the robbery, a relief mission had been dispatched from the branch office at Selwood to retrieve the vehicle. There had been no damage to the wheels or axles, so a fresh team of sand mares had been attached to drive the armored coach to the head office where a more thorough inspection could be conducted.

Myles Ferguson picked through the coach's interior, seeking to identify everything that had been taken. The fortune in gold dust was obviously gone, though he hoped that the other cargo remained in place. Fiddling with the secret panel at the back of the safe, he slid open the compartment to find it empty. A surge of dread pulsed through him as he considered the sort of criminal who'd take interest in the odd object that had been concealed there.

"What's the matter, dear?" a woman's voice asked after Myles cursed under his breath.

"It's gone," Myles said. "The *item* has been taken." He stepped back and tried to slam the heavy metal door of the safe, though the weight was too great and the hinges were too dry to do more than budge it. Frustrated, he set his hand on the hilt of a saber he always carried, as if intent to cleave the damaged lockbox. It was only a fleeting thought, and he left his blade sheathed.

Myles left the stage and went over to the woman, his loving wife, Nora. She didn't say much as he approached, but she stared at him with those big brown eyes that could peel away the layers of a man's soul. Her quiet nature made her seem pretty standoffish to strangers, as she had to Myles not so long ago. But the years had brought them together, and now she was the most important thing in his life, above and beyond the company he and his cousin had built.

Nora reached out and placed her hands on Myles' shoulders when he was within her grasp. "Don't worry about it," she said. "We can always refine more."

Myles shook her consoling hands away. "That's not the point, is it?" He turned and looked at the stage, seeing the metal plates of its armor peeled back like crumpled paper. "Who could have done this? How did they know where to look, and what possible interest could they have in that special metal? Can you answer me that?"

Nora remained silent.

There was a chilling breeze coming out of the west, something odd for this sunny spring day; a bitter harbinger of the troubles ahead. Myles tried to shake it off as his own nerves, but it was too clear there was more to it than that. Whoever had robbed this stage was no petty bandit out for ill-gotten riches. No, they were far too powerful for that sort of thing, and that they had taken the half-sphere of radioactive ore alluded to their advanced knowledge base. It was a scant few in this world who knew of the true power of that poisoned metal, and fewer still who would desire it.

As the chill wind grew stronger, Myles felt it wise to head inside, though his wife remained still. He took her arm and tried to urge her toward the loading bay of the warehouse, but she did not budge. She stared up into the western sky intently, as if peering through the pale blueness into the darkness of space beyond. "I can't move," she whispered as the wind began to howl.

Myles felt his flight instinct kicking into overdrive, urging him to run from this place, though he couldn't leave. His grand lineage demanded that he stand firm, and there was Nora to consider. She wasn't budging, and he couldn't abandon her, so his resolve was steeled, whatever the consequences.

Braving the cold sting of the air currents, Myles stood beside his wife until everything stopped. One instant, the icy gale was about to knock them over, and the next it was warm and stagnant again, as it had been a minute before.

Time itself seemed to halt, as Myles looked around the open lot. He took a step away from Nora and turned around in a full circle, searching for someone or something that he knew must be there. Whatever had caused the wind couldn't be far away now; more likely the adversary was watching him! That frigid wind show was a bit of theatrics, the sort favored by the more flamboyant wizards.

Obviously, the metal wasn't all the thief was after.

A flash of light streaked out from a patch of thin air not fifty feet from where Myles stood. Instinct spared him from the brunt of the mystic bolt, but the graze scorched his suit jacket. He tossed it to the ground in a smoldering heap and drew his saber, prepared to face his enemy with courage.

"Stand forth, warlock!" Myles shouted into the air. His voice reflected against the brick buildings on three sides of the loading yard, causing an echo.

A sinister laugh answered his challenge, and after a few seconds a figure appeared in the yard, dressed in black. Tobias Sylvestri was enjoying himself, smiling as he approached the sword-wielding merchant with thinning hair and a slight paunch of an overgrown belly. There wasn't much menacing about Myles; at least, not in the warlock's eyes.

"Get back, you shyte!" Ferguson snapped as Tobias came within reach of his blade. After the last word was spoken, a golden glow emanated from the blade, and the warlock's progress stopped as his face met an invisible barrier. Myles jerked the blade twice, and with each motion the invisible barrier pushed against the warlock's face, moving him backwards.

The smile melted off Tobias' face, and with an angry thought he dispelled the barrier, but as he tried to move toward his target, again he found a hardened patch of air blocking his progress. The tangible force then expanded, wrapping itself around his body, locking him in place. Such trickery was to be expected from this man who'd formerly owned the radioactive metal. It was clear he possessed great knowledge of the ages, knowledge even beyond that of the Guild.

"If you intend to harm me, you'll taste my blade," Myles challenged, pointing the tip of his sword under the warlock's chin.

Tobias blinked, and in that instant his mind examined the energy patterns around him.   He sensed the waves of magic coursing through the sword, and the effect that energy was having on the air in front of him. It was easy enough for him to formulate a more permanent counter to the spell, though he decided to let his opponent think him powerless against the restraining field. Some people are more boastful from a position of strength, willing to reveal things they ordinarily would keep to themselves.

"Who are you," Myles snapped.   "What are your intentions here?"

"My name is Tobias Sylvestri," he said, sounding pleased with himself.   "What I want is the man who created the hunk of poisoned ore which I removed from your safe."

The admission was plain enough, so Myles knew without doubt that he was face to face with the murdering bandit responsible for the stage coach robbery. Questions still remained, concerning the warlock's interest in the metal and what he had planned for it. Was this man even of this Earth?

Eager to get some answers, Myles asked.   "Why are you interested in the ore?"

"One question," Tobias countered.   "What did you have planned for that hunk you were transporting in the stagecoach?"

"I would ask the same question," Myles replied.

"You were shipping it somewhere," Tobias said, ignoring his opponent's query. "Where was it going? Not Selwood, that would be too obvious. Kingman, then? Milford, perhaps?"

So, he knew the company's branch offices. That did Myles little good in seeking to understand this enemy. This wasn't getting him anywhere, and it was time to put an end to it. This warlock wouldn't cooperate, and whatever his true intentions for the metal, they'd best be stopped. There was only one sure way to do that.

The color of the blade's energy darkened until it was nearly black. Myles raised it high and proclaimed. "In the name of Wallace, I send you to your master." He swung the blade, intent on beheading Tobias, but as it reached the warlock's neck, the metal struck an impenetrable barrier. The impact sent a painful shock through Myles' arm, and in an instant he knew he was once more in peril.

Shaking off the effects of the restraining field, Tobias stepped forward and yanked the sword from Myles' grip with a magic command. Slapping a hand around the man's neck, Tobias remarked, "A Knight of Wallace. How quaint. I thought your lot had been wiped out with the Jacobites."

"You'll get nothing from me," Myles replied. "Dispatch me and be done with it."

"How noble of you," Tobias said with continued amusement in his voice, "and also revealing. Your willingness to die for your secret tells me it is worth knowing."

Myles felt the sting of mental intrusion, of Tobias peeking into his thoughts. The curious sensation was very familiar to Myles, and as a Knight of Wallace he had mental barriers in place to deflect such probing. No telepath on this Earth had yet been able to break through the mental discipline of the modern knights, though there was no telling where this warlock was from. Was he merely a man, or something far worse?

After a grueling minute of intense concentration, Tobias withdrew his mental probes and tossed Myles to the ground. Keeping his cool, he said, "Well, I guess we'll just have to do this the hard way."

A coil of fire rose up from the ground and wrapped itself around Myles like a blanket. The mystic flames licked at his skin but did not burn in any noticeable, physical way. Despite the outward appearance, however, the sensation of burning stung at Myles, and each moment was more unbearable than the last. The sense of being cooked alive was not only excruciating, but terrifying beyond measure. He couldn't help but scream.

As the pain grew so great that Myles was certain he'd die from it, the flames receded, leaving him without a mark. He breathed a sigh of relief as the world around him returned to its regular calm.

"Now you know what awaits you each time you lie to me, or refuse to answer," Tobias said.

The momentary relief was shattered by the statement, as Myles feared his own human weakness. That few seconds of agony had been enough to break any man. How could Myles stand another taste of it? Yet, how could he reveal the secrets he held?

"First question: who made the half sphere?"

"I don't know," Myles said hastily, clinging to the last vestiges of courage.

In response to the non-answer, Tobias brought back the coil of fire and scorched Myles for several seconds, just enough to make him regret the deception.

Myles staggered to the ground as the magic receded. He fought to stay on his knees as his muscles stung and knotted from the aftershock. The magic may not have left any outward marks, but there was no telling what internal damage it was causing.

"I may not be able to steal your thoughts, but I can still sense your intentions. Lie to me again, and you'll suffer far longer."

Despite the pain, Myles stood up, unwilling to remain on the ground, beneath his enemy. He would face the man eye to eye. Both legs felt like pins and needles, and throbbed with each heartbeat, yet he persevered.

"Again, who made that hunk of poisoned metal?"

"I did," Myles answered.

"Hmm, half true," Tobias said, eyeing him suspiciously. "You had others help you, no doubt the miners and machinists who work for your company. However, were you the mastermind behind the metal's refinement?"

"Yes, I alone instructed them to..."

The magic flames returned again, and this time they lingered on Myles' body for twenty seconds, leaving him screeching like a banshee. There was no way he could stay on his feet under such pain, though the magic field kept him standing until the fires receded. He collapsed in a crumpled heap onto the cobblestone paving.

"Interesting," Tobias remarked as he waited for his subject to regain enough strength to speak again. "Of course, you're not the creator. You're just the guardian knight, doing his job. So, who are you protecting? Who's really behind the metal's creation?"

"I will not tell you!" Tobias shouted defiantly.

Tobias raised his hand, ready to scorch the man again.

"Stop!" Nora shouted, rushing over to Myles on the ground. She'd been watching the conflict, unable to intervene. She had no power to repel the warlock, and could do nothing but stand silently and hope that her husband could prevail. Yet, there was only so much she could take, and seeing Myles in such agony was an intolerable emotional strain on her.

Sensing another avenue for answers, Tobias shot his mental probes at Nora, only to find them turned back with greater force than any he'd felt before. Her barriers were beyond what even the Knights of Wallace could form, enough to block any intrusion whatsoever. Another piece of the puzzle was revealed.

"You want him to live, you will answer," Tobias said, as Nora cradled the exhausted Myles in her arms. "You had the metal refined, didn't you?"

"Yes," Nora replied with bitter resentment.

"Then you can make me more," Tobias said. It wasn't a question, but an order.

"Why?" Nora asked. "What possible use could you have for it?"

"Ah, but that begs the question, what use could *you* have for it?"

Nora didn't answer immediately, but looked at her husband, seeing the worried look on his face. He had been willing to die to protect her, and the expression he gave told her he wished he had been given that chance. The truth was far too dangerous to be revealed.

Tobias responded to Nora's silence by summoning the mystic fire once more. The spiral of flame wrapped itself around Myles and Nora together, paining the man, but leaving the woman unscathed. After a few seconds, the warlock rescinded his spell.

"Please, stop it!" Nora pleaded.

"Then give me what I want!" Tobias commanded.

"You don't know what you're asking. You can't," Nora said, almost in tears.

"My conjuring may not affect you, but your husband will suffer if you don't obey me. I swear I'll kill him!"

"And how many more will die if I give you what you want?" Nora asked.

Calming down, Tobias stepped forward, to be closer to his captives. "I'm not interested in hurting anyone, but I have no choice."

"There's always a choice, Tobias," a deep voice answered.

Tobias turned around seeking the owner of the new voice, and spotted him, sitting inside the mangled wreckage of the stagecoach. The leather-clad man with dark hair and a badge pinned to his chest was vaguely familiar to the malicious warlock, though immediate identification was difficult.

"Is this any way for a Master of the Guild to behave?" the man asked as he sauntered over.

"I'm no Master," Tobias replied, keeping half an eye on his prisoners as the new foe approached. "I never completed the exams."

"You're still the son of the Guildmaster, aren't you? Tobias Sylvestri, heir to the vaunted throne of the Wizardry Guild's West American chapter. How low you've sunk."

As the man came within arm's reach, Tobias recognized the face. "James Doliber, isn't it?"

"That's right," Doliber replied. "You tutored me in spatial displacement at the academy. Long time no see."

"Sheriff, eh?" Tobias remarked, reading the badge. "So, my father stooped so low as to call in the law on me."

"I'm here on my own," Doliber admitted. "Your father did his best to dissuade me from pursuing you. Obviously, he's not willing to chance what might be necessary to bring you in."

"More likely he's too ashamed of me to let my behavior be exposed to the collegians. Imagine the stigma, to be the father of a murdering bandit."

"There's more to it than that, and we both know it," Doliber said, hoping to get some answers before their meeting deteriorated into violence.

"There always is," Tobias mentioned rhetorically.

Growing weary of chit-chat, Tobias stepped back and swung his arm in a roundabout manner, creating a glistening arc of magic force. The thin blade of energy streaked through the air, and Doliber's neck was the intended target.

By the time Doliber knew what Tobias was doing, the magic was already released, and he was too close to avoid the impact through ordinary, physical reaction. Working on instinct, the sheriff cast a metabolic accelerant spell, allowing his body to move far beyond its normal constraints. By his perceptions, time around him slowed, while his body remained mobile. The shimmering blade of magic glistened a few inches from his neck, crawling toward him in a blurred ripple. It was already too close for him to run out of the way, so he relaxed his knees and let himself fall backwards. There was just enough time for him to hit the pavement before his perceptions returned to normal, and the deadly bolt of energy flew away, slapping against a brick wall in the distance.

Seeing his target's tricky maneuver, Tobias grimaced in frustration.

"I'm not a plucky young apprentice anymore, Toby," Doliber said, straightening up.

Tobias wouldn't be mocked, and responded with a new spell, one that Doliber couldn't avoid. The paralytic field enveloped the sheriff in an instant, and it appeared to do the trick. Doliber squirmed and shook, attempting to break the invisible bonds, but to no avail.

"Never call me *Toby*," Tobias said with bitter disdain. Adjusting the restraining field with a mental command and a ceremonious tightening of his fist, he forced Doliber onto his knees. "You were such a promising cadet, James. It's a shame you abandoned your calling to play law man."

"Funny," Doliber said, gasping against the tightening field. "Your father said the same thing."

Tobias tightened the field further in anger, squeezing Doliber into silence. "Do not test me today, Apprentice. I have no qualms about killing, and you know it."

Doliber struggled to speak, so Tobias relaxed the field to hear his answer.

"We aren't really that different, are we?" Doliber replied. "We've both taken issue with the Guild leadership, and their politics. The only real difference is the manner in which we've rebelled."

"You have no idea," Tobias replied, taking a step back. It was time to end this distraction, and get back to his original purpose. Focusing his thoughts, he strengthened the field around Doliber, and prepared to enact a lethal squeeze.

As the field began to crush him, Doliber unleashed his true counteragent, preventing the powerful magic from squashing him into a bloody pulp. As his own mystic field pushed against Tobias' lethal restraint, he shouted, "Now!"

A blurry figure suddenly caught Tobias' eye, and he turned just in time to see an elvish woman standing beside him. Before he could do more than identify her, she tossed a cloud of red dust in his face. He'd been too focused on the antagonizing sheriff and keeping track of the Fergusons to detect the presence of this magically-shrouded enemy.

It had been a clever gambit Doliber had played, Tobias thought, as he felt the numbing dust soak into his body. When the magical substance penetrated his cells, it worked as a narcotic, shutting down his mental functions. If he'd realized it a second sooner, he might have been able to conjure a counteragent to the elf's enchanted chemicals, but it was already too late, and his eyes grew dark as a curtain of slumber came upon him.

As Tobias fell to the ground, his wicked magics vanished. Doliber stood up and rubbed at his chest, checking to make sure his ribs were still solid. "That was close," he mentioned, regaining his bearings.

"I've yet to meet a human magician who can dispel Essence of Red Moon," Joella replied, wiping her hands on her chaps. She was looking very masculine in her attire, despite her pretty face.

"You've never challenged a master of the Guild before," Doliber rebutted. "You may have pride in your elvish mysticism, but it is not infallible. We should feel lucky it worked on someone of Tobias Sylvestri's power."

With the threat neutralized, Doliber turned his attention to Myles and Nora Ferguson, who remained much as they'd been throughout the conflict, seated on the ground, patiently waiting for the next shoe to drop. Walking over to them, Doliber offered his hand, and Nora graciously accepted his help.

"Thank you, Sheriff," she said, springing nimbly to her feet without trouble.

Doliber offered Myles a hand, but the knight would accept no assistance. Instead, he staggered to his feet, struggling against the lingering effects of the magic assault. It was impossible for him to hide all the pain he was feeling, but he bore it well.

"Your help has been much appreciated, sir," Myles said as he straightened up. "Now, if you'll excuse us, my wife and I had best be off."

Doliber was about to protest, but Myles added, "Don't worry, we'll be sure to make ourselves available to testify at his trial."

It wasn't all he had wanted, but Doliber was willing to leave it at that. He would have his hands full interrogating Tobias in a few hours. Answers from the Fergusons could wait for a later date.

As Doliber turned to leave, Nora called him back. "Wait."

Myles grabbed Nora's arm gently. "What are you doing?"

"What I must," Nora answered. Stepping forward and placing a hand on Doliber's chest, she said, "Sheriff, I sense you are a man of honor, and quite obviously significant talents. Do you also possess an open mind?"

"Sometimes," Doliber replied, curious to know what would follow.

Myles urged her back and whispered, "Nora, you can't. He won't understand."

"We must trust that he will," Nora said.

"We can't."

"What's the alternative? Wait for whoever sent this renegade warlock to show up in person?" Nora shook her head. "I know you want to protect me, but our circumstances have changed. We need help."

Myles bowed his head in shame and looked ready to cry.

"Sheriff, we must speak in confidence, away from prying eyes and mystic eavesdropping," Nora said.

"That can be arranged, but I'd better take care of this first," Doliber said, turning to the unconscious Tobias. Joella had done a good job of tying him up, though the knots would hardly hold a skilled warlock. The bonds would only work in conjunction with other, more ethereal restraints that would neutralize his mastery over magic.

A specially modified prison cell could contain Tobias, or so Doliber hoped. Either way, his next stop would be the sheriff's office in Selwood, to stow this most deadly criminal for the interim.

* * *

Ron Grimes fiddled with the two-page newspaper from the Selwood Star Tribune. It was a mild diversion as he sat behind the sheriff's desk, holding down the fort while Doliber ran off with Joella to catch some magic bandit. It seemed a bit much for Ron to believe; that someone from the illustrious Guild would stoop to robbing a stagecoach. Either way, a dwarf had no place in the field of mystic combat, so here he sat, babysitting.

Ron finished reading an article about a proposed rail-line spur for the Selwood area as a grunt caught his attention. Putting down the paper and hopping out of the chair, he walked over to the open archway a few steps away from the desk, which led to the holding cells. The office doubled as the town jail, which is how Doliber liked it, and in residence was Brian "Buck" Gormley.

Buck was a slim Englishman with long, brown hair and a few loose teeth. His alleged profession was carpentry, though nobody local had ever seen him drive a nail. He'd been spending the last few months at the Lucca Saloon, getting drunk and playing cards. He'd had a pretty good streak going, earning enough to pay his bar tab and visit the ladies upstairs on occasion, but that all ended when Solen the barkeeper caught him cheating. Nobody cheated at Solen's Faro table except Solen, and the dispute ended in a brawl.

Doliber's decision had been to place Buck Gormley under arrest for disorderly conduct. Now, Ron was here to greet the man as he woke up.

"Bloody Hell!" Gormley shouted as he struggled to sit up on the cot. Growling, he rubbed both hands over his face, as if trying to rub off the top layer of skin. There were a few bruises on his left cheek and he flinched as he stroked them.

"Enjoying your stay?" Ron asked, stepping in front of the cell door.

Gormley blinked nervously and stared at the short figure on the other side of the bars. "Hey, I know you. You're that midge what shot the half breed elf a while back."

"That's right," Ron said.

"Well, good," Gormley said, standing up to stretch. "No place for scum like that in civilization, is there?"

"You're one to talk," Ron remarked. He had no sympathy for

drunken card cheats, British or otherwise.

"What's that supposed to mean?" Gormley asked, sounding insulted.

"It means you're lucky the sheriff didn't let Solen take his losses out of your hide. Rigging a game's as good as stealing in my book."

"I rigged nothing," Gormley defended. "How could I? I wasn't dealing."

"The sheriff said you were popped for cheating, and that's good enough for me," Ron answered, turning to leave. He'd satisfied his curiosity and it was time to reread the newspaper for the third time, or maybe play with a few of the new lever actions sitting in the gun cabinet. Doliber had told him to leave the hardware alone, though his boredom was bordering on madness. That was a good enough excuse to examine the ordnance, right?

"I say, Deputy," Gormley said, walking over to the bars as Ron turned away. "Are you simply going to leave me locked up in here, alone? Aren't I entitled to a lawyer?"

"Don't look at me. This is my first day on the job," Ron said, slowing his pace. Something told him he wouldn't be escaping the Englishman's chatter.

"Oh, isn't that typical," Gormley complained, leaning an arm against the cell door. "This is supposed to be such a just land. *Innocent until proven guilty,* and all that. Bollocks, I say."

Ron turned and glared at Gormley, wondering how the cocky fellow had lived so long without being lynched. His arrogance seeped through with every word, and it rubbed Ron the wrong way.

"If you weren't already locked in that cell, I'd put you on your ass," Ron snapped, stomping back over to the cell door. A little voice in the back of his mind said, *'open the door, and give him a good whupping,'* but he couldn't. He'd given his word to safeguard the man, and above all else Ron was honorable.

Gormley stared down at his jailer, and asked, "Wouldn't you like to hear my side of the story?"

Ron felt like laughing, but kept his cool. "This has to be good," he said, deciding it would provide a momentary distraction.

"I'm not the one who was rigging the Faro table," Gormley

began. "That dirty elvish barkeep had been doing it long before I arrived. He was shaving cards, playing both ends against the middle, so I foolishly made him look the fool by winning more than his dealer. Since the dealer knew how the cards would fall, and bet accordingly, it wasn't hard for him to conclude that I had to have an equal, unfair advantage. So, I was rousted."

"You sure did win a lot over the past months. How'd you do that on a rigged table?"

"I never play Faro. Not normally. It's a simpleton's game, with no true skill required. No, I'm a poker man, but when I saw them cheating the Faro players, it seemed only appropriate that I cheat the house as retribution."

Ron smiled and fought back a laugh. He wasn't sure if it were true, though it sounded good. "So, how'd you do it, really?"

Gormley stopped for a second and patted his shirt, searching for something. Finding the appropriate pocket, he withdrew the remains of a pair of glasses which appeared to have been stepped on. The lenses were gone, and the wire frames were bent to be hardly recognizable. "Penetrating spectacles, revealed the top few cards. I suppose some might call it cheating, though it's certainly justified against true scam artists, don't you think?"

The story didn't quite ring true. Oh, Ron had no trouble believing that Solen was rigging his games, but Gormley had been in town for months, raking in a tidy sum at cards. This man had been using those spyglasses at all the games in town, stealing people's money through his own dirty tricks. It was sickening, though the fact that Gormley had been doing it for months without anyone catching on left Ron scratching his head. "How'd you get away with it for so long?" he had to ask.

"I played fair, that's how," Gormley said, oozing with pride. "Cards are my forte, and that is how I have avoided hard labor in America. Fine gambling establishments you Yanks have here, I must say. I'm not generally a trickster, though when I saw chicanery afoot and I'd had a few drinks, somehow the notion of showing them up seemed a clever idea. Suppose I should have stayed at the poker table."

"Right," Ron said, feeling he was the one being *played*.

"I fully intend to explain this all to the magistrate... er, judge, as soon as a hearing is convened. You wouldn't happen to know when that's liable to happen, eh?"

"Like I said, it's my first day," Ron said, turning to leave. He'd gotten as much entertainment out of the prisoner as he felt appropriate, and thought it high time he examined those lever guns.

The gun rack was sitting on a conspicuous patch of wall behind the sheriff's desk. Inside there sat half a dozen serviceable rifles, ranging from an old Henry Repeater to a first year 1873 Winchester. As useful and reliable as those were, they weren't nearly as intriguing as the slim, wooden box leaned up in the far right. The crate was branded "Marlin Repeating Arms Co."

Ron had heard about lever actions capable of firing high powered cartridges. He'd even had the chance to try an 1876 Winchester last year during a skinning job in the Dakotas. It had dropped him a buffalo, though the strength of the round still hadn't equaled the single shot Sharps he'd also been able to sample. The latest news running through the hunting journals spoke of a Marlin lever action capable of handling the .45-70 Government cartridge. That was a gun Ron had to see.

Ron grabbed the chair behind the desk and stood on it to reach the light chain hanging in front of the gun rack. Reaching in to grab the box, he felt the tingle of anticipation, as he prepared to behold a powerful piece of hardware. The weight of the box sent a wave of adrenaline through him, like a kid at Christmas, eager to open a mysterious present.

"Deputy Grimes, what are you doing?" a voice asked.

Ron hastily put the box back in the rack and turned to see Sheriff Doliber standing behind him, along with Joella and an unconscious man dressed in black. Such an inopportune time for them to arrive. Couldn't they have waited a minute longer?

"I was just checking on things," Ron replied.

"Get that box down here and open it up," Doliber said after an awkward silence. "We might be needing some firepower before long."

"Right!" Ron exclaimed, turning back to get the box, failing to realize how foolish he'd appeared a moment earlier. That a grown dwarf would have such childish feelings over a mechanical instrument should have made him feel ashamed, but he didn't.

Ron grabbed the box and set it on the desk as Doliber made his way over beside him.   Joella simply carried on, dragging the unconscious prisoner over to the cell block.

As the crate made contact with the desk, the sheriff reached over and streaked his fingers against one side in a curious fashion. "There, now you can open it," he said.

The action was very telling, and Ron understood why Doliber had told him to keep his hands off the box. It had no doubt been enchanted somehow.   There was no telling what would have happened had he tried to open it without the sheriff's permission. Working for a warlock was something to get used to. You never could be sure what mystic trickery was in use.

After sliding a couple of clasps off their hitches, Ron raised the lid and pulled back the paper packing to reveal a shiny, nickel-plated rifle.   The long, octagonal bore glistened, and the thin receiver left him in awe. He'd expected something more bulky and cumbersome, but this fine thing looked lighter than a '76 Winchester. What a marvel of modern mechanical theory!

"So, what do you think? Was it a good investment?" Doliber asked.

Raising the rifle to his shoulder, Ron looked down the iron sights and remarked, "Sure could've used one of these when I was fighting them werewolves earlier," Ron remarked.

"You survived," Doliber replied, taking the rifle from the dwarf. "Don't see how you can handle the length of the stock with those arms."

"My legs may be short, but I've got reach," Ron replied, feeling a tad insulted.

Doliber cycled the action and dry fired the weapon, sampling the trigger-pull. It wasn't as smooth as a Winchester, he thought, but it was still a fine weapon, with a lot of power. He could appreciate its potential, even if any halfway decent magician could deflect its lethal shots. There were only so many "decent" magic users, even in this modern day and age of advanced educational standards. Besides, there were some augmentations he could add to the ammunition, to assure the weapon's usefulness against mystically endowed opponents.

"Grab a box of shells, and come on," Doliber instructed,

leaning the rifle against his shoulder.

Ron complied, and then followed Doliber into the cell block. Both men walked over to Joella, who was unlocking the last barred door. The tarnished key rattled in the lock, even as a glint of silver light sprayed out of the keyhole. As the key completed a half-turn, a beam of light dropped from the ceiling, trickling down the bars until it hit the floor and vanished. With the special cell opened, Joella grabbed her prisoner and tossed him inside, slamming the door shut behind him. He lay there on his face as she reinserted the key. When the door was locked, the magic restraining field was restored with another ripple of light.

"Think this will hold him?" Joella asked Doliber as she handed him the key.

"There's no telling what'll hold him," Doliber replied. "How long is that dust of yours supposed to last?"

"Twelve hours, at least," Joella answered.

"I'll be back within six," Doliber said. "In the meantime, keep an eye on him, and make sure the crooked gambler doesn't get lynched."

"Hey!" Gormley cried from his cell up the block.

"Oh, no, you're not leaving me behind now," Joella protested.

"You wanted to be deputized," Doliber reminded her. "You've got the job, at least until I get back." With a clever wink, he turned around and waved his hand, teleporting away in a flash of light, and taking Ron with him.

Joella folded her arms across her chest and pouted. "Of all the arrogant..." she mumbled to herself.

As Joella walked back toward the sheriff's office, she caught Gormley staring at her. She paused momentarily to shoot the prisoner a narrowed stare, which looked especially vicious with her naturally upturned eyebrows.

"Say, Miss, would you happen to know when they serve supper around here?"

Joella hissed at him and stormed over to the sheriff's desk, where a chair awaited. As she sat down, she saw a newspaper poking out from under the heavy wooden crate sitting on the desk; a little light reading to pass the time. She yanked it free and saw the totality of the sheet with disappointment. So few words for a newspaper. At least, the limited content would hold her for a few minutes. Where was a good book when she needed one?

* * *

Myles was still sitting on the ground, working the knots out of his legs as Nora stood and watched him. There was an awkward silence, as they waited for the return of Sheriff Doliber.

"I tell you, this is a mistake," Myles mentioned when he could not restrain his opinionated mouth any longer.

"What part?" Nora asked.

"You really plan to tell that warlock your secrets? He's an ignorant savage."

"As were you, dear husband, before I educated you," Nora reminded him.

"That's different," Myles rebutted. "I am a Knight of Wallace, trained to be attuned to the higher plains. Your revelations didn't surprise me."

"Liar," Nora said, clearly amused. She stopped and giggled a little, enjoying a moment of levity in the midst of dire circumstances.

Myles shook his head and stood up, fighting to keep his balance. Both legs still ached, and any movement brought worse pain. It would be difficult to walk, but he was determined to try. Taking a few steps forward, the muscles locked up, forcing him to stumble. Nora rushed to catch him before the paving stones could break his fall.

"Oh, let me go," Myles complained in vain. Nora wasn't about to let him be hurt any further, and there was no way he could carry his own weight at the moment.

"You don't have to try so hard to impress me, Myles," Nora consoled as she supported him. The man was easily twice her weight, but she didn't struggle against his girth. Her muscles were well developed, though you'd never tell from the frilly dress that hid her body.

"That's not the point," Myles grumbled. "I swore an oath, even before our marriage, to defend and protect you. What good am I if I can't do that?"

Nora snorted in a less than ladylike fashion. "Do you think I married you to be a glorified bodyguard?"

Myles looked at her deep brown eyes, then turned to face the ground. "The thought has crossed my mind."

"It hurts that you could think so little of me," Nora replied, sounding sincerely saddened.

"That's not it at all. It's no reflection on you. I understand you had to make do under the circumstances, trapped in this place, alone. But, honestly, look at the world we're living in. This is where I'm from. It's a part of who I am, and I can't change that. Even if I'm more enlightened than these primitive fools, I must still seem a barbarian compared to you."

"Oh, no," Nora said. "You don't at all. Not anymore. I married you because you are a good man, a kind and honorable soul. You can be stubborn at times, but that's what makes me love you so much."

Myles lightened up after her gentle words of comfort. "I'm your noble savage, am I?"

Brushing a hand over his thinning hair, she said, "We do not choose our place of birth, but sometimes we can choose our destination."

"Do you really think the sheriff will help us?"

Nora didn't answer, leaving Myles with his misgivings. There was no way to predict how Doliber would react to the other-worldly explanations that awaited. As steeped in superstitious mysticism as warlocks were on this Earth, could one accept a greater truth beyond their training, and how would he react if he didn't?

Episode Seven:
The Bastard Revealed

Tobias Sylvestri found himself enveloped in light. The glow came from all around him, even the spongy ground beneath his body. He was lying face down in a mossy substance that could hardly be seen due to the brightness it exuded.

Staggering to his feet, Tobias tried to figure out where he was, and how he'd gotten here. No answer came to him, as he fought to recount what had happened.

He recalled the loading yard outside the Ferguson and Finney building; the amusing knight and his enigmatic wife. He recalled the warlock sheriff who'd interrupted his quest, and then the elf, the very female elf. A puff of red dust numbed his cheeks and nose...

Now, he was here, in this land of light. How strange.

A shadow caught the corner of Tobias' eye, but there was nothing except that pure light for as far as he could see. Or was it illumination at all? Who's to say blindness is always dark? Had his eyes been left invalid with that dust attack? He couldn't tell, for he'd never experienced anything like this before.

Another shade flew past his right side, and he jerked back to catch a glimpse of it, failing yet again. He spun around in a circle, finding nothing. Was his mind playing tricks on him, as well?

There was another explanation that floated across his mind, and with an instinctual thought he sought to cast a spell, one designed to augment his eyes and give him the ability to perceive enchantments. When cast properly, the spell would allow his eyes to see objects saturated with mystic energy, thus revealing most anything hidden or disguised by conjuring.

Nothing happened.

The lack of results disturbed Tobias more than anything, for there should have been a response to his command. Even if the spell had failed to manifest, there would have been a residual sensation in the back of his head, from the part of his mind that manipulated the mystic ether. Yet, he felt nothing. It was as if he had been stripped of his ability to command magic altogether, which was theoretically impossible. Such a conscious reflex could not be wholly removed. There were stories from ancient times of Roman Legionnaires cutting out hunks of sorcerer's brains to stop their spell-casting, though it was only a foolish old legend, little more than a fairytale.

"What have they done to me?" Tobias asked the light around him, his heart surging with apprehension.

"Nothing," an echoing voice replied.

Tobias wasn't accustomed to such flippancy in that voice, but he recognized who was speaking. "Sage? Where are you?" he asked as his fear ebbed.

"Where you left me, in the cavern," the sage replied, sounding amused. Strange, the man had never been very jovial in the past. What had him so elated?

"Then where am I?" Tobias asked.

"You're in a holding cell in Selwood, a prisoner of that joke of a sheriff and his deputized minions," the sage replied, sounding more serious. "They drugged you, and there you lie, unconscious."

"Curses!" Tobias snapped, stomping his foot at the glowing mush beneath him. He now knew where this was, an ethereal plain of existence, outside the physical world. The "astral plain" as some scholars called it. This realm was one of pure thought, only accessible to skilled mentalists and certain exotic animals. He'd never visited this place before, and could only imagine the sage had brought him here purposely.

"Nice place you've brought us to," Tobias added, staring at the glistening light that floated around in cloud-like splotches.

"I've always taken solace in this place, a world beyond human consciousness," the sage mentioned. "Here, one can experience their pure essence, beyond physicality. You should be grateful that I brought you here, if only for a moment."

"I'm honored," Tobias said, trying to set aside his emotions, but finding it difficult.

"It would be more advantageous for you to ponder your own failings, which landed you in such a predicament as this."

"Yeah, thanks," Tobias said, feeling slighted. "About my circumstances, can't you do something?"

"Oh, I am doing *something*," the sage replied with a sinister inflection. "At this very moment, I am preparing to finish something I started long ago, all thanks to you. As shameful as your performance was, you did well to locating the ultimate prize, or at least the individuals capable of delivering it to me. You have my sincerest gratitude."

"I'm glad you're happy," Tobias grumbled, feeling like the butt of a joke. *'I can't believe I let myself be caught. This is embarrassing,'* he thought.

"On the contrary, you should be glad they captured you," the sage mentioned, having read his mind. "It saves me the trouble of having to kill you."

"What?" Tobias exclaimed, shocked by the sudden betrayal. "But we had an agreement!"

"Please. Can you make a deal with a horse or an ox? You were little more than a beast of burden, doing the work I was unable to perform. You have served your purpose, and your usefulness is at an end."

"You swore to God Almighty that you would return my wife to me!" Tobias shouted with clenched fists.

"Farewell, Tobias. Be comforted in the fact that I did not reunite you with your fallen bride. Better to live alone than not to live at all."

The sage's voice grew silent, and Tobias screamed, unable to contain his rage. All he had worked for, everything he had done, was for nothing. He'd poisoned his own soul, murdered and stolen as a means to an end, and now he was left betrayed. He couldn't see the justice in his defeat, only an overwhelming sorrow at knowing his wife would never return, and an unquenchable thirst for revenge against the man who had used him.

If he could ever find a way back to his physical body and break free from the sheriff's cell, he swore he'd find the sage and put him in the ground, permanently.

* * *

Ron Grimes was greeted by a warm breeze blowing down his neck, a disconcerting thing to feel in the dark. Teleports were disorienting enough without being dumped into the unknown like this. Until recently Ron had had the pleasure to avoid such mystic transportation, and part of him still wished to return to more traditional means of getting around. Horses existed for a reason, and two legs could make up a lot of ground. Still, there was only so far a man could move in that fashion, and when time was of the essence, it was handy to have a warlock as your ace in the hole.

After spiriting away from the sheriff's office, Doliber had introduced Ron to the Fergusons. The couple seemed plain enough, so Ron couldn't guess why a mystic bandit would be after them. Were they really that rich? No, there was more to it, they assured him, and to prove their claims and answer questions Nora offered to deliver them to something that would speak louder than words. She provided Doliber with spatial coordinates via a telepathic jolt, something Ron could scarcely understand, and without another word they were off.

Now they lurked in the dark.

"This is the place?" Ron grumbled, looking around, trying to make out faint objects. His eyes were adjusted to broad daylight, so the gloom of the room prevented immediate identification.

"These are the coordinates you gave me," Doliber said to Nora, even as he calculated the distance in his head. He guessed they were somewhere in southwestern Utah, though a precise location eluded him. He was taking a big leap of faith here, trusting that Nora Ferguson wasn't leading him into harm's way.

"Indeed," Nora replied. "Come, there may not be much time." She moved along slowly, helping Myles to limp along. She clearly knew this place, for the dark didn't bother her movement in the least.

Doliber's eyes flashed momentarily, as he amplified his vision with a spell. He offered to augment Ron's vision in a similar manner, but the dwarf refused, wary of mysticism despite the possible advantage.

"Suit yourself," Doliber said, starting to follow the Fergusons down the hallway. "Hey, hang on to this," he added, tossing the 1881 Marlin rifle to Ron.

Catching a flying weapon in the dark was not one of Ron's skills, but he managed to grip the hunk of wood and metal with only a few bruised knuckles. The pain quickly subsided, and it did feel good to have the great equalizer once again in his grip. The fine lever action was a step above the Remington revolver at his hip, and would serve him well if they ran into unforeseen trouble.

Ron tagged along behind everyone, as they ventured down a long, narrow hallway. He tried to stick to the center, to avoid hitting various objects hanging on the walls. He thought they were paintings, though he couldn't see enough to tell.

As the floor changed to a gradual decline, Nora asked, "How do you perceive your world? Do you think of it as singular in nature, unique and separate from all else in creation?"

Ron opened his mouth to ask, "Maybe you'd like to run that by me again?"

"I was speaking to your sheriff," Nora said dismissively. "So, tell me, what do you believe, Master Warlock?"

"I'm a Journeyman," Doliber corrected, "and if you're asking about my faith, I can assure you I've slept through my fair share of sermons."

"Then you are a Christian man? How peculiar."

"What do you mean?" Doliber asked.

"That someone who dabbles in the mystic arts would follow such a doctrine."

"All powers in Heaven and Earth are sourced from the Creator. Christ himself 'dabbled' as you so aptly put it, so the Guild sees no contradiction in its members following His teachings."

"I take it you're not a Calvinist," Nora remarked.

"I'm His, never mind the denomination," Doliber said.

"And what of you, little man?" Nora asked. "Do you share your sheriff's devotion?"

"My folks raised me Dwarf Orthodox, something of an offshoot of the Greek. Can't say I've followed it much lately."

"Why not?" Nora asked politely.

"I'm not one for all the holier than thou preaching and philosophical conjecture. Seems to me what matters to a man is what he can make of himself in this life, never mind the next."

"Are you an atheist, then?"

"I didn't say that," Ron corrected. "I think there's a God, but I don't waste my time trying to figure him out, that's all."

"I see," Nora said. "Then I take it neither of you believes in the multitude of worlds."

"Say that again?" Doliber asked, as Ron made a similar request.

"Let me show you," Nora said, stopping her pace as the hallway ended. The way in front of them was blocked, and in the gloom the faint outlines of a rectangular door was barely visible. Nora reached for a small panel beside the door which opened the way. As the door lifted, a bright light shone from the room beyond.

"Welcome to your future," Nora said as they stepped forward into the spacious chamber.

Blinking against the light, Ron fought to see the splendor of the enchanted room. It was not like anything from his imagination, with metal pipes and cables running all along each wall. Crystal coils dangled from the ceiling pulsing, and multi-colored light throbbed from them like a beating heart. In the center of the room sat a raised dais with many pedestals and chairs jutting up around a central pillar. All along the pillar were glowing cubes and rectangles, some with words and pictures displayed behind sheets of glass.

After a moment of awe, Ron shook it off and masked his wonder with skepticism. "Quite a display of magic tricks," he said, equating them to something his mind could comprehend.

"Hardly," Nora replied as she helped her husband into a yellow chair. The smooth material of the seat made a swishing sound as his clothes rubbed against it, and Ron moved over to touch the backing. It had the feel of varnished wood, but it was wafer thin.

With her husband resting comfortably, Nora walked toward the central pedestal. "This technology is powered by non-magical forms of electricity. It is the product of pure science."

"Electricity is one of the five primary energies according to spell-casting theory," Doliber said, hurrying over to her side.

Nora smiled at his comment, "A very archaic assumption."

"The five primaries are a well known fact," Doliber defended. "Heat, Electricity, Kinetics or Motion, Gravity, and Magic. Are you saying there are more?"

"What you perceive as separate forms of energy can all be linked via Unification Theory. Though, I don't expect you to understand the higher points of Quantum Mechanics. It would be like explaining gunpowder to a caveman."

Doliber grabbed her arm and turned her to face him. "Enough of this. You asked for my help, and said there were answers to be had."

"There are, but first you must accept that there will be some answers beyond your ability to understand."

"It seems you are playing me for a fool," Doliber said, almost shouting.

"No, I am simply trying to ease you into this, so you'll be more accepting of the truth," Nora said, cool and collected.

"Enough," Doliber said releasing her arm. "Out with it. Why was Tobias after you, and why do you need my help? What's really going on here?"

"As you wish," Nora said resignedly. "Come, let us sit." She walked over to a cushioned chair placed in front of a glowing rectangle hanging from the central pillar and invited Doliber to take another, identical seat beside it.

As they got settled, Ron walked over, keeping his eye half on Nora and half on the strange equipment that glistened with the colorful words and symbols. He wasn't going to be left out of things, not after being dragged along as Doliber's backup. There was something unnatural about all of this, and he kept his hands wrapped around the Marlin rifle, prepared to raise it at a moment's notice.

Nora folded her hands and set them on her knee, taking the pose of a thoughtful lecturer. "Where to begin?" She paused and looked at a few of the glowing screens, while steeped in contemplation. "What would you say if I told you I was not of this world?"

Doliber hesitated, as he considered the possibilities. What other worlds were there, he pondered? Before he could think it through, a new voice answered for him.

"Quite simple; he'll ask if you are from Heaven or Hell, or some other mythical realm his limited mind can relate to."

The sound had come from the open hallway, and all eyes turned to watch the owner of the voice walk into the room; a small, unassuming man with white hair and wrinkled brow, dressed in gray robes. From all appearances, he was a harmless, little old man, though appearances were so often deceiving.

Myles rose from his seat and unsheathed his sword. "Halt in the name of Wallace!" he exclaimed, seeking to quell the shiver in his aching muscles.

The old man's response to the knight's challenge was a literal slap in the face. Casting a spell, the man knocked the sword into Myles' cheek, the flat of the blade hitting hard but not lethally. It would leave a nasty bruise, for certain.

"As for the rest of you, I wouldn't waste time threatening me with your novel trinkets," the old man said. He walked further into the room, approaching the great dais with its many technological wonders. As he passed Ron, he gave the dwarf a nasty sneer.

"Who are you?" Nora asked calmly, "and why are you here?"

"I should ask you the same question," the old man said. "Though, I'm sure we can both figure it out."

"You're the one who sent that warlock after us," Nora concluded. "The one who is after uranium."

"How very perceptive of you," the old man said. "But to answer your first question more precisely, I am Mortimer Blythe."

Nora's pleasant demeanor was instantly dashed, as the familiar name stung at her memory. A look of abject dread flowed from her forehead down, like a falling curtain. "Blythe the Bastard," she whispered in terror.

"Guilty as charged. My mother was never the marrying type," Mortimer said with a courteous bow.

As the initial exchange was taking place, Doliber was hard at work, seeking to gain an advantage. Sending out his mental probes, he tried to peek into the mind of this new adversary, though the attempt proved useless. Never before had he encountered a mind so impenetrable, so guarded against intrusion. He couldn't read a simple emotion, let alone a complex thought.

"Are you finished?" Mortimer asked, turning to the sheriff after horrifying Nora with the truth of his identity.

"Apparently," Doliber replied.

Turning around to face the dwarf and bruised knight, Mortimer said, "I trust you're both smart enough to realize that resistance against me is futile." Turning back to face Doliber and Nora, he added, "It's time to cooperate."

"No," Nora said, pushing back in her chair, as if an extra inch of distance from Mortimer could make a difference.

"And who are you to refuse me, little girl?" Mortimer asked.

"I am no one you'd know," Nora said.

"Probably not, but I assume we're from the same world, or one of them, at least."

The cryptic banter was driving Ron up the wall, and as the enigma became too burdensome, he had to interrupt. "Would somebody mind explaining what the hell is going on?"

Mortimer turned on his heels to face Ron, and simply stared at the dwarf. There was an unspoken hatred lurking between them both, something almost instinctual. Each knew the other was their enemy, and wished for an excuse to make the first move, though neither did.

"This man is a monster," Nora finally said, breaking the staring contest. "He's wiped entire worlds from existence."

Mortimer turned his attention back to Nora and blushed. "Such praise from a lady. Oh, it's been too long. Allow me to reciprocate. You have my thanks for your assistance."

"I will not help you," Nora said defiantly.

Mortimer smiled and leaned over her. "My dear, you already have."

The room went dark. In an instant, the light vanished, every bit of it from each of the glowing screens and crystals. The absolute black caught everyone by surprise.

Doliber was the first to react, creating a glowing ball of fire which he left hovering in the air above him. The magical flame provided a dim light, not nearly as powerful as the technological devices had extruded, but it was enough to see by.

Mortimer was gone.

Nora leaned forward, and rested her face on her opened palms. She allowed her feelings to burst to the surface, as the sting of defeat ate at her soul. All she had worked for was about to be unraveled, and it was her own fault. If only she'd been more cautious, things wouldn't be so dire. Her own desires had overcome her better judgment, and played into the hands of the most dreaded of enemies.

"That was really Mortimer Blythe?" Myles said, limping over to his wife. The knots in his muscles were still significant, and he used his sword as a crutch.

"Yes," Nora said, wiping her eyes.

"But it can't be," Myles said, stepping on the dais and stumbling forward. He caught himself on the arm of Nora's chair, and slumped against it for support. After recovering, he continued. "What are the odds of him being here, of all worlds?"

"I knew it was a possibility," Nora said. "There are a limited number of quantum passageways linking each reality. Of the few thousand possible permutations, it's clear that Mortimer and I came down the same one."

"I'm gonna pretend I understood that," Ron remarked, looking around the room, waving the rifle in the air. He wished for a target, an excuse to test the deadly weapon. If that tormenting Bastard reappeared, he'd gladly take a shot at him.

"He defeated me," Nora said tearfully, leaving her head lowered.

"We're not beaten yet, my love," Myles said, putting an arm around her shoulders. "This mad warlock hasn't seen the best of us yet, right lads?" He turned and looked at Ron and Doliber, both men giving him a reassuring nod.

"Oh, no," Nora said, raising her head to expose tear-soaked cheeks. "He is no mere warlock. More like Satan Incarnate. When I call him the destroyer of worlds, I mean it. If we don't stop him, you will not have lived to face the consequences."

"Not have lived?" Doliber asked, catching the curious wordplay.

"Precisely," Nora replied, lifting her head to face him.

Though her eyes were swollen, there were no tears. "Mortimer Blythe and I both come from another world, another Earth that existed en-tandem with this one, only in a separate quantum state. Please, it would take too long to explain the complexities of the multiverse, so take my word for it, and let me continue.

"The people of my world were technologically advanced, centuries ahead of what you know. Mortimer Blythe was an accredited scientist, whose own brilliance got the better of him. He was employed by the Ministry of Science to unlock the secrets of temporal mechanics—time travel. The end result of Mortimer's research was the Negative Engine, a device capable of manipulating matter at the temporal level. With it, Mortimer has the power to affect the life of a single atom or an entire planet. Quite literally, if he gets his way, your world will never have existed, and none of you will ever have been born."

"That makes no sense," Ron complained. "If he has this power, what's the point of wiping everything out?"

"His methods aren't always clear, though on our homeworld, he only did it after a demand for ransom was declined by the world's governments."

"And what were his demands?" Doliber asked.

"Absolute reign over the entire world; a global dictatorship. Nobody thought he would really follow through on his threat until it was too late. A few others like myself may have escaped, but I'm the only one I know about."

"Other than Bastard Blythe," Myles added superfluously.

It was a lot to swallow, and Doliber didn't know how much of it to believe, though he didn't doubt the severity of the situation. If even part of Nora's claim was true, something had to be done to stop this Mortimer Blythe, and quickly. No man could possess such life destroying power as he was purported to have, so the logical response came. "What's our next move?"

Nora held up her hand for silence, as she looked around the room, as lifeless as it all was. There was no power to run her equipment any longer, and she was still guessing at the reason why. Mortimer had either pulled the fuel cells, or possibly the entire reactor, no doubt seeking uranium to revive his Negative Engine. The thing required a controlled explosion to work, much like her Gateway device that burrowed through quantum layers to connect divergent realities. That's how he had found her in the first place. He'd somehow detected her last shipment of uranium while it was in-transit.

Yes, her own wandering desires had bested her. If she'd been content to live in this backward world for the rest of her life, none of this would be happening. She'd have grown old with Myles, happy and safe, yet it hadn't been enough. Living in a world that was just inventing the light bulb was too primitive for her, so she'd strived to revive her Gateway generator, and seek out another alternate Earth, one where they at least had a few computer chips under development—somewhere she could serve a purpose again.

Instead, she'd handed a monster the means to destroy another world.

There was no time to sulk and wallow in guilt. She had to figure out a way to correct her mistake, and stop the one man in all the worlds that she truly hated. It wouldn't be easy, and she didn't know if there was enough time to succeed, but she would try. In the end, that's all anyone can do.

A thousand variables flowed through Nora's head, as she searched for the answer.

Seeing the three men standing around her, she politely said, "Let me think for a minute, and then we'll get to work."

"Do we have a minute?" Ron asked, storming over with rifle in hand. There was little reassurance in holding the shiny weapon, but at least he could pretend for the moment.

"Yes, we have time," Nora said, snapping back to life with a hint of optimism in her voice. "It'll take him time to calculate the proper chronol wavelength to disperse your entire world, and longer to charge the Negative Engine for the task."

"How much time?" Doliber asked.

"A few hours I expect," Nora said. "That's the best guess my research team had come up with before..." She trailed off, as memories of her own world flowed out. It still hurt to think about it; the world that had never been.

"Then we have time for an interrogation," Doliber said, straightening up and walking away. He waved at Ron, and the dwarf followed dutifully. "We'll be back once we have some answers. Then, maybe, we can formulate some kind of coherent plan," the sheriff added as he reached the gloomy entryway.

* * *

Ron and Doliber arrived at the sheriff's office as they had left, abruptly and unannounced. Joella jumped to attention as the two men appeared in a flash of magic, eager to hear what they had learned during their short absence. "That was quick," she remarked.

Doliber placed his hands on Joella's shoulders in a gentle but impassioned manner. "Listen to me, this is important. Is there any way to neutralize the sleeping dust you gave Tobias? We need him awake in a hurry."

"Of course," Joella replied, digging into a hidden pocket sewn into the side of her pant leg. From it, she produced a tiny pouch. "A few particles of this should do the trick."

Doliber took the little pouch and loosed the string to open it.

"Oh, don't get any on yourself," Joella advised. "It's very potent."

Doliber turned for the cell block, with Joella and Ron following. "You'll have to tell me where you get this stuff sometime," he remarked.

"There's an alchemist in every elven village," Joella replied. She spoke as if he were being absurd. Everyone knew the source of elven powders, surely. Would he make the same remark if a Chinaman handed him a bottle of laudanum?

As they walked to the cell, Doliber got a funny feeling. The slightest trace of telepathic residue was lingering in the air, a scent he found familiar. It wasn't the sort of thing he would have ordinarily noticed, and not something a skilled mentalist would have left behind without a good reason. The intruder had wanted him to know about the intrusion, but why?

Doliber unlocked the prison cell as his mind picked over the purposeful clue. Whoever had been here had no doubt come about Tobias, and may have invaded his thoughts. The nature of their conversation was something the sheriff could only imagine, and he hoped it would prove useful at this critical juncture.

Walking over to the limp figure lying on the floor, Doliber shook a few particles of white dust out of the bag and watched them drift down to the slumbering figure. The magic substance glistened brightly as it made contact with skin, and within moments Tobias began to stir.

With a groan and a stretch, Tobias rolled into a sitting position tugging at the rope which restrained his hands behind his back. Doliber removed the bindings and offered him a hand, but Tobias stubbornly slapped it away, and stood up on his own.

"It's time for some answers," Doliber started.

"Oh, it's time for much more than that," Tobias corrected. "It's time for retribution!"

Doliber stepped to the side, and Ron leveled his rifle at the man in black, prepared to shoot him dead if necessary.

Tobias put his arms up, but kept an angry expression on his face. "I didn't mean you. The sage! He's betrayed me!"

"You just stay right there," Ron said as Tobias stepped toward the open cell door.

"You must believe, I mean you no harm," Tobias said. "Not now."

"You expect us to trust you?" Ron asked, keeping his aim steady.

Doliber darted out of the cell and looked back at Tobias, who appeared harmless enough. The energy field within the cell prevented warlocks from utilizing their powers in any way, by assaulting the part of their brains that cast spells. Variations of the jamming field had been utilized for centuries, but it was never infallible, and this particular cell had never been tested against a full-fledged Guild member. Yet, if Tobias were able to circumvent the field's power, he made no attempt to do so.

Once outside the cell's influence, Doliber's brain unlocked, and he cast the spell to send his mind wandering. Following the lingering traces from a previous telepathic intrusion, he entered Tobias' mind and reviewed the conversation he'd had with "the sage," otherwise known as Mortimer Blythe. The mental image was plain in Tobias' thoughts, but there was something wrong; a residual mental signature which Doliber recognized.

After reviewing the short exchange Tobias had had with the mock Mortimer Blythe, Doliber realized someone was playing a trick here, but it was one the sheriff could certainly use to his advantage.

"Satisfied?" Tobias asked, as Doliber's perceptions returned to physical reality.

"That's not a term I'd use," Doliber answered, glancing over at Ron. "Lower the rifle, Grimes. I don't think he'll jump us."

"Are you kidding?" Joella asked.

"Would I joke at a time like this?" Doliber asked. "The entire world is about to blow away. What's the worst he could do to us?"

"If I might make a suggestion," Tobias said, stepping forth from the cell. "You shouldn't be asking what I might do to you, but what I could do to the sage *for* you."

* * *

At last, the time had come. Another world, another version of Earth, was about to end. Better still, it would never have been.

Mortimer Blythe looked at the metal pod sitting on his work bench, the outer casing to a fission generator filled with radioactive fuel. The rods wouldn't be the right shape, but it wouldn't be hard for someone of his proficiency to adapt them to his purpose. There was enough power there to erase this planet from existence, and punch a hole to the next for his timely escape.

How many worlds had ceased to be at his hand? Twenty seven, he recalled. It wasn't hard to keep track, as every day was a constant reminder of his successes and limitations. The cycle had been ongoing for all the centuries of his life, far longer than anyone would suspect.

Each world was different, and the time it took to acquire the necessary components for a Negative Engine varied, based on the level of technological advancement for each human race. If not for the unexpected presence of a sophisticated refugee in this backwards realm, it might have taken him decades to manufacture the fuel he required. How ironic that someone from the last world he destroyed would be his key to destroying the next.

What a bother that last one had been. A race almost as advanced as his own, with technology capable of thwarting his mission; it had been the most precarious erasure he'd ever conducted. It had required much subterfuge, and a lot of role playing to trick the natives into thinking him a harmless madman, rather than what he truly was.

So many copies of the same world: so many pale imitations of the Prime Earth of his origin.

Mortimer could scarcely remember his youth, so many centuries into the past. Growing up in the glistening cities of glass, experiencing the height of modern science and magic. His people had advanced to a state of near perfection in their view, wiping out disease, hunger, and providing peace and order across the globe. It had been paradise.

Then the war came.

It was a conflict like none other, a clash of worlds. Invaders came down from the skies, at first thought to be extra-terrestrial, but their true origins turned out to be far stranger. They were men from Earth, only a quantum variant. Scientists had ruled the possibility of alternate realities to be a theoretical improbability ages ago, so it had come as quite a shock to battle such an enemy.

Caught off guard as they were, Mortimer's people had feared themselves doomed from the start, but their salvation came with yet another unexpected discovery. The invaders had no understanding of "trans-quantum energy," no mastery of magic. Their brains had not developed to manipulate matter in such a way, and that left them at a grave disadvantage.

The invaders had soon found themselves on the defensive, fleeing for their lives in the face of a million trained mages. During the retreat, the would-be conquerors lost significant assets, including various quantum tunneling devices. Thus, the key to inter-dimensional travel was delivered to the people of the Prime Earth.

Mortimer had been a young recruit in the mystic militia during those fateful weeks of warfare. It had been so long ago, it was becoming a blur, though he would never forget his purpose, to assure it never happened again. These myriad worlds could not be allowed to threaten the stability of the one, true reality ever again. So here he was, taking pre-emptive action.

"How long must I suffer these pathetic copies?" Mortimer mused as he cut the casing of the fission generator with his magic finger. He destabilized the atomic bonds in a straight line, so he could remove the metal shell in several large plates.

It was no easy task to quash the rise of alternate Earths, but

Mortimer was not alone in his quest. Following the creation of the Negative Engine, hundreds of brave men and women like himself had voluntarily departed from his world to map the multiverse, and erase any world-be threat. Each had their own definition of "threat" and he had no way of knowing how the others were progressing, so he had to keep going, relentless in his quest. "If you want something done right, do it yourself."

It could take an eternity, but Mortimer was determined to collapse the continuum of alternates, and assure his own reality's supremacy for all time.

The casing came off, piece by piece, revealing a complex web of wires and conduits. The configuration was a bit primitive, as Mortimer would expect, though that didn't matter. All he cared about was the fissionable material in the core.

Enhancing his sight with a mystic trick, he was able to see the different energy waves coming from the deactivated generator. There, in the heart of the device, was a square block with various pipes and wires sticking out of it. Peering deeper beyond the metal shielding of that box, he saw the radioactive waves within, and smiled in appreciation. His goal had been achieved, at last. His mission on this pathetic world was nearly over, and he would soon start anew on another alternate Earth.

The lives involved never crossed his mind. It wasn't murder, after all. How can you kill something that never was?

Episode Eight:
The Negative Engine

The vast cavern was aglow with the pure light of incandescent bulbs. Such a far cry from the relative gloom of the best oil lamps, not to mention candles. The brightness underground was something beyond what Ron had expected to see in his days. A few years back, he would have chalked it all up to magic of some sort, but since word of Edison's fantastic innovation had spread, the dwarf now understood there was physical science at work instead. Not that there wasn't science behind magic, also, but this electrical illumination worked on wholly different principles.

The sound of machinery echoed through the rocky cavern, the clicking of gears and the hum of motors in the distance. They gave him a clear path to follow, one that he hoped would lead him to the man he sought, the most vile and villainous being from another world.

Ron walked cautiously through the spacious room, toward the large altar cluttered with metal bits and pieces; the remains of different devices from a realm of high-technology and futuristic wonders. He glanced at the curious things in passing, wondering what could be made of them. Would anyone from this world have the slightest inkling of what to do with the strange remnants? If so, what possible impact could they have on the future? Would it make much difference either way, or would man progress at a pre-determined pace, regardless of the inventions?

Ron shook his head. Such philosophical conjecture was best left to the idle intellectuals, he thought. Why was he wasting time with such ponderings? There was a job to be done, so he'd best get on with it.

Exploring the back of the cavern where the light was weak, Ron found a passageway tucked behind a bookcase. The sounds of machines were definitely coming from down there, so down he went, ignoring the thumping in his chest, but hanging a hand in the vicinity of his holstered pistol in case it could serve him.

"All right, folks, here goes," Ron whispered as he walked down the slightly sloping hallway. It started out as the same smooth stone of the cavern, but as he came to a bend, the natural surfaces turned to steel. There were several sharp turns in the hall, as he continued toward the noise, and he eventually saw what had to be the end. A straight stretch of a hundred feet ended at a hazy blur. The overhead light let him see clearly as he walked up to the magical barrier. What lay beyond was anyone's guess, though he'd soon find out.

The closer Ron got to the blurry barrier, the stronger the distortion appeared. Fuzzy waves rippled across the surface periodically, as the field replenished itself. He couldn't tell if the barrier was merely an illusion to hide the room beyond, or if it had actual substance. One touch could reveal the truth, but such action could prove fatal. Many a mystic field held a lethal charge, and Ron was ill equipped to discern if this one posed such a threat.

This would be a defining moment; a simple step forward to test his courage. One simple move with his hand outstretched would leave no doubt about the field's properties. Whether he lived to tell of them was another question entirely.

The fate of the world hung in the balance, so now was not a time for cowardice. He had to press on, whatever the consequences.

After a brief hesitation, Ron put his hand up and pushed it through the glowing field, feeling stinging pain pulsing through his muscles. The sensation was like thawing frostbite, something Ron had had the displeasure to feel once. Though, this was all rushed. The pain of an hour's thaw was being forced upon his hand in an instant as it passed through the barrier, though it stopped as soon as he pulled it back. Wiggling his fingers, he found them to be unharmed. Except for the memory of pain, he was unaffected.

Seeing he could survive the field, Ron took three steps forward and forced his entire body through. The freezing-burn of the field flashed over him, and he found the pain overwhelming, far greater than he'd hoped. It forced him to collapse in exhaustion, even as the pain was replaced with numbness. The shock had left him paralyzed!

Ron blinked his eyes as he fought to regain control of his appendages. Now was no time to be caught lying down on the job, but the muscles weren't responding. Little twitches were all he could muster, leaving him staring at another metal wall.

Ron's eyes and ears were still in working order, so he could hear the footsteps coming toward him. As the soft clicking grew dangerously close, he managed to twist his neck around, and stared at the strange, black moccasins resting beside his head, and the thin ankles sticking out of them.

"Well, this is amusing," Mortimer said in his cold, calculating voice.

"Didn't expect to see me again, eh?" Ron asked, as he continued to struggle with sleeping muscles.

"You're clearly here as a diversion," Mortimer deduced. "As foolish a ploy as it may be, I'll give you credit for determination."

As his muscles remained unresponsive, Ron felt himself being lifted off the floor. A bit of Mortimer's magic elevated him until his legs were dangling several feet in the air, and he hung face to face with the madman from another plain of existence.

"So, what are your friends up to?" Mortimer asked, glaring into Ron's eyes.

"Go to Hell!" Ron growled defiantly.

Mortimer didn't reply with words, but sent a tormenting spell, and a new burst of pain filled Ron's mind. The torment began in the center of his head, and shot out like a thousand hot needles poking at his skull. The sensation lasted for only a few seconds, followed by a wave of relieving calm.

"Now, cooperate and spare yourself any more misery," Mortimer advised.

"All right!" Ron cried, doing his best to sound defeated. "I'll tell you everything, just leave me alone!"

"Good," Mortimer answered. "Be honest. I'll know if you're

lying."

Ron wasn't sure how true the statement was, but he didn't need to lie. That was the beauty of his role in the plan.

"You want the truth?" Ron whispered. "Look behind you."

Mortimer turned around right as Joella appeared out of thin air to blow red dust in his face. Though the plan was fairly similar to the one they'd used against Tobias, it did not succeed against the sagely madman. As the elvish powder touched Mortimer's skin, he quickly neutralized it with the barest magical effort.

"Pathetic," he said, sending a debilitating burst of wind at Joella with a flick of his wrist. "Did you really believe such an amateurish trick would incapacitate me?" he added as Joella was slammed against the floor.

"Hey, it worked before," Ron mentioned as he continued to hover in mid-air.

"Yes, I saw what you did to my apprentice," Mortimer mentioned, turning back to face Ron. "Can't you think of anything new?" Clenching one fist, the madman sent the magic needles back into the dwarf's head. "How pitiful; your limited imaginations leave you recycling the same strategy over and over again."

"Yeah, we're just so predictable," Ron struggled to say as his brain felt ready to melt.

Mortimer sneered at Ron and tossed him to the floor. He had clearly had enough of the playful banter. As he turned to walk away, Ron sought to hold his attention. "Hey, you know why we keep using the same tricks?"

Mortimer ignored him and kept walking, but suddenly stumbled as a bolt of invisible force snapped his legs.

"Because they always work," Ron answered.

As Mortimer rolled into a sitting position with two broken legs, he began to laugh; hardly the response Ron had expected. The agony alone would generally preclude the ability to find humor at such a time, but Mortimer was no ordinary man.

"Ah, Sheriff Doliber," Mortimer said, glancing around the room, searching. "I was wondering when you'd make your presence known."

Ron managed to pick himself up off the floor, though it hurt like hell. Back on his feet, he stood and stared at Mortimer, watching him grinning as if his injuries were all a big joke.

"So, are you going to show yourself?" Mortimer asked the sheriff. "No? Well, perhaps a little something above your grade level may convince you to be more sociable."

A pale blue glow suddenly emanated from Mortimer's legs, and moments later a scream sounded from the far side of the room. Sheriff Doliber appeared in a gloomy corner, his mystic invisibility defeated as his concentration failed, and he collapsed to his knees.

When the azure glow dissipated from around Mortimer's body, the madman stood up with two healed legs. He walked over to his would-be disabler and kicked him hard in the shins. "Metaphysical reversion. Transposes my injuries onto you, while healing me."

Doliber cried in agony as Mortimer kicked him again.

"You fools think you can compare to my power?" Mortimer asked viciously with outstretched arms. "My people mastered mysticism while you were still living in caves. We built cities with mysticism beyond your comprehension, and merged it with technology to achieve a level of utopia!"

"Our world was hardly a utopia."

Ron turned and saw Nora entering the room from the same hallway he'd come through, though unaffected by the shimmering barrier. He didn't understand how she could be so resistant to the field, even though her magical abilities were virtually nil. Perhaps it was the long, fur coat she wore, or perhaps her race was truly different from the humans he knew.

Mortimer locked his eyes on Nora, and watched as she approached with short and cautious steps.

"Ours was a world of chaos, a hundred monarchs fighting for supremacy. Very few were as benevolent and enlightened as our own Queen Victoria." Nora stopped within arm's reach of the madman, her hands tucked into her coat pockets.

"Speak for yourself. I have no queen," Mortimer rebutted.

"Of course not. I imagine a man willing to annihilate an entire world would crown himself monarch, in his own mind," Nora goaded.

"Your superstitions were your greatest failing," Mortimer said with conceit. "That technologically superior beings would willingly bow down to a feudal monarch makes me sick! There is no divine right of kings." He looked over her shoulder toward Ron. "Isn't that right, Mr. Grimes?"

"Sounds about right," Ron said, finding it odd that he'd agree with the madman on any topic.

"So," Mortimer said, casting his eyes upon Nora again. "Even the primitives of this America understand such a basic truth. What does that say about you?"

"It is not about truth, Bastard," Nora cursed. "It's about honor and civility, two things you have clearly never known."

Brushing open her coat, she drew a dagger from her belt and thrust it in Mortimer's direction. The madman caught her wrist before the blade could stab into his chest, but he struggled against her strength. There was no magic being used, purely physical muscle, and Ron had to question the meaning of the battle. If Mortimer Blythe was such a powerful wizard, couldn't he overwhelm Nora in an instant? Why were they wrestling?

Nora slapped her other hand on her wrist, fighting to push the dagger into her foe. He countered with a double grip of his own, though it only made for an even match. Neither had the upper hand in physical combat, which made things unpredictable.

"Where's that worthless husband of yours?" Mortimer asked. "Still cowering in shame, playing the wounded knight?"

"Sir Myles is a braver man than you'll ever be," Nora snapped. Shifting her stance as they danced around the dagger, she lifted her leg and kneed Mortimer in the crotch, causing him to cringe. The shock weakened him enough to give her the advantage, and she plunged the blade into his waiting chest.

Mortimer pushed Nora away and staggered back. Yanking the blade from his chest, he tossed it to the ground and waved his hands over the wound, managing a partial healing job. He hissed in anger as blood continued to trickle onto his shirt. "A piece of your world, I see," he said, hurling a red beam at the blade. The magic ray struck the dagger, but didn't affect it in the least. Frustrated, he redirected the beam at Nora, but it was equally useless against her.

"The sorcery of this world cannot affect me," Nora said as the red light dissipated against her. "Not unless I wish it."

Their bout was clearly over, as Mortimer stood on the losing end, brushing a hand over the bloody stain on his shirt. The wound underneath the soaked cloth was still red, though the majority of the cut was sealed. He grumbled in frustration, then vanished in the blink of an eye. The teleport had been seamless, with no noise or light distortion; the sort of perfect displacement only performed by warlocks of the highest order.

With Mortimer gone, Ron rushed over to check on Joella. She was still breathing, though didn't wake to his light prodding. There was a lump on the back of her head where it had hit the floor, though nothing seemed to be broken. As he stood up after checking her over, he felt funny that he cared so much to worry. A few days ago, this woman had been his adversary, an opportunist who had kidnapped him for her own ends. Now, he had to admit they were growing toward genuine friendship.

"How is she?" Doliber asked.

"I think she'll be okay," Ron replied, looking up to see the sheriff standing over him. "Looks like I can say the same for you."

"Yes, the wounds Mortimer inflicted weren't as deep as I led him to believe," Doliber said.

"That was some good acting," Ron mentioned, standing up. "Ever think of doing a stage show?"

Doliber put on a halfhearted smile. "It was nothing compared to Nora. That bluff was brilliant. We're just lucky Mortimer was too flustered to tell I was deflecting the beam before it could burn you."

"True, but past experience aided the deception," Nora explained. "You must understand, these clothes and the dagger are from my world, which resonates at a far denser wavelength than your own. Magic energy cannot affect matter from my universe as easily as it does yours. Mortimer knows this, so I knew he'd rationally believe my resistance to magic could be amplified."

"After this is all over, you'll have to explain it to me nice and slow," Doliber mentioned, looking around the room. It wasn't much to look at, really; metal walls and some furniture, like a giant bank vault turned into a living room.

"It's quite simple, if you can grasp the basics of String Theory," Nora mentioned. "In essence, my world was made up of subatomic particles that resisted quantum manipulation, so magic was virtually unheard of."

"Now, wait a minute," Ron said, struggling to understand. "You're saying stuff from your universe is immune to magic. If that's so, how come you teleported with the rest of us?"

"I've spent the past five years here, remember? Eating the food, breathing the air, absorbing the molecular structure of this world; my cells have slowly adapted to this reality. Inanimate objects seem to adapt to their surrounds as well, though not as quickly, which is why my dagger was able to harm Mortimer and leave enough molecular residue to hamper his healing spell."

"So, you become a part of the world you live in," Ron surmised.

"Essentially," Nora said. "I imagine that's how Blythe was able to learn the use of magic. As his cells adjusted to this world, he was able to tap into the divergent quantum energies you people take for granted."

"I don't think so," Doliber said, kicking over a small end-table for the satisfaction. "You've both been here what, five years? I've been studying magic my whole life, and I'm not as powerful as Blythe. And there was something he said, about his world building cities with magic and technology. That doesn't fit what you've told us of your origins."

"What are you suggesting?" Nora asked, sounding scared by the implications.

"Maybe Mortimer Blythe was as much an outsider to your world as he is to ours," Doliber suggested.

Nora shuddered at the concept, and an eerie silence fell upon them.

Ron didn't let the idea bother him any more than he was already bugged. The whole situation was convoluted, with truths and theories that flew way over his head, so he tried to keep things simple. They'd had a job to do here, and one important question remained. "Do you think we stalled him long enough?"

"We can only hope," Nora replied. "And trust that your instincts are correct."

Doliber nodded, wondering if he had made the right decision, though what other option had there been? Time was short, and the only chance at success lay with another kind of madman.

The key to victory hinged on the will and proficiency of Tobias Sylvestri, the former accomplice of Mortimer Blythe. Tobias was the most unscrupulous sort, someone who had seen fit to commit murder when it offered to benefit his cause. Would a man so easily swayed by self-interest follow through with his part, or falter at the final hurdle?

* * *

The fate of the entire world was bearing down on Tobias as he paced around inside Mortimer's inner sanctum. The underground chamber was cramped, and filled with dangling wires and bright lights, along with a conspicuous control panel filled with buttons and switches. What was it Nora had called it? The Negative Engine? Not much to look at, Tobias thought. All those people he'd killed, all the chaos he'd inflicted, had been to create this pathetic little room.

Tobias cursed and punched the wall, infuriated by his own actions, and the ultimate betrayal. Mortimer had promised him so much, and taught him such horrible things, all with the promise that Sarah would be returned to him. His beloved wife, the victim of his intense studies, was truly dead for all time.

Blythe the Bastards had merely capitalized on his sorrow, and turned him into a soulless destroyer.

Tobias remembered what it was like to care. Though meditation and training had taught him to eliminate the weaker emotions from his mind, it was impossible to delete the memories. The man Sarah had loved was not the man he had become. Self examination made him realize how wrong it all had been, this vain pursuit of a dead dream. Even if Blythe's offer had been true, and Sarah could have been revived, what would she have seen in this new man who'd been created to save her?

Tobias had betrayed his love. Worse, he had almost betrayed the entire world. This Negative Engine held the potential to erase everyone from existence, or so Nora Ferguson claimed. If even an inkling of her accusation were true, this weapon had to be destroyed. It was a matter of self-preservation.

Deep down, Tobias knew he had no hope for redemption; not in his mind, anyway. All he had left was revenge!

Pulling himself out of his introspective trance, Tobias stared at the control console, and with a magic eye peered beyond the colorful lights and switches to see its inner workings. He beheld the complex wiring and carefully laid circuit boards that comprised the brain of the engine, and saw beneath it all the beating heart. The power core was heavily shielded, but beyond the thick casing the faintest traces of radiation could be detected by the warlock's extraordinary senses. He'd seen this poison before, resonating from the half sphere of metal he'd stolen from the stagecoach. Uranium, Nora Ferguson called it.

That deadly metal was the source of Mortimer's power. How satisfying to take it away from him!

Tobias stretched out with a thought, seeking to perform the same neutralizing spell he'd cast on the half-sphere, to eradicate the radioactive properties of the metal. Try as he might, he couldn't get through the casing. The physical and mystical defenses in place were too great. He would have to get closer.

Removing a wrench from his pocket, Tobias knelt down and began to remove the bolts holding a service panel in place. The bolts unscrewed easily enough, but after the plate was free and he opened it to expose the inner working, a blinding flash burned his eyes. How foolish he felt, having fallen for such a predictable trick.

No bother, Tobias thought, as he cast a rejuvenation spell to restore his sight. Nothing! He tried again to restore his vision, but try as he might, the magic would not work. Whether his vision was gone for good he couldn't tell, but for certain it was not coming back immediately. He'd have to work around it.

Using the mastery he held over his own mind, Tobias recalled the mental image he'd seen of the console's inner workings. Looking back at his memory of the device, he was able to superimpose that vision over his blind eyes, and see where his hands were situated. Moving around the wires and circuits, he reached for the oblong metal pod that sat at arm's reach from the access panel. Touching it, he could sense the power within. It was invigorating to feel such energy, so primal and pure, unlike any he had ever sensed before. This was beyond magic. It was the essence of reality itself he felt.

What a shame to destroy such naked power, Tobias thought. Surely, there was a way he could harness it for himself, and do right with such a force. To take this power from the man who had used him, wouldn't that be all the better? Truly, his revenge would be twofold!

Yet what would he become if given such power? Would he be a benevolent god, or a wrathful monster? He knew the answer, and for the first time in years he understood what his father had said all those years ago. A true Master must know his limitations, and that does not always mean the limits of one's power, but of one's ability to utilize such power responsibly. The greatest warlocks in history had been far more powerful than they allowed themselves to be, simply because they understood the darkness in their own souls.

That moment, Tobias knew what he must do. Casting his spell, he punched through the anti-magic wards and neutralized the energy waves coursing within the metal pod, removing the lifeblood of the Negative Engine. As the nuclear fuel reached a state of depletion, the console went dim, and the rhythmic hum of the devices grew silent. The threat was ended.

Crawling out from under the console, Tobias heard an impassioned shout. "What have you done?"

Turning to face the voice, Tobias knew that Mortimer Blythe, the enigmatic sage, was standing right in front of him. "You're finished," Tobias said bitterly. "We're finished."

Mortimer's heart was filled with rage. His servant had betrayed him! That had not been foreseen. His plans were quickly turning to ashes, and he could hardly believe it. "How dare you turn on me! To think, I was going to bring you with me to the next world, where your wife would be waiting for you!"

"Lies!" Tobias growled in response. "You never had any intention of resurrecting my wife. All this time you were building this thing to destroy the world."

"That's only part of it! I had every intention of fulfilling my end of the bargain, only not as you would understand. It no longer matters. We aren't going to the next world where your wife awaits. We can't go anywhere!"

Tobias charged at Mortimer and slammed him against the wall. Even blind, he could still sense the man's presence, and pretend to see. "I know your game now, Sage. You turn on me when you think you're ahead, but when the chips are down you think you can trick me into your wicked web again!"

"By God, what are you blithering about?" Mortimer asked.

"Our little conversation on the astral plain. You thought I wouldn't remember? How you mocked me!"

"I did no such thing!" Mortimer defended. "Don't you see they've played you? Nora Ferguson and that meddling sheriff have used you to destroy all that we'd accomplished." Mortimer grabbed Tobias by the collar and shook him.

Tobias broke free from the grip, and tossed Mortimer back against the wall, but it wasn't long before the elderly sage had the upper hand. A magical bolt tossed Tobias away, slamming him into the powerless console. The buttons and switches dug into his shoulders as Mortimer continued to exude magical force against him.

Tobias felt it was the end. His body was being crushed, and there was nothing he could do to stop it. He had exhausted his spell casting abilities, and Mortimer was too powerful. This was a less than satisfactory end, and his revenge was incomplete. He screamed against the pain, more out of frustration than agony.

Then, suddenly, the pain stopped.

Mortimer Blythe groaned and coughed, as Tobias straightened up, feeling the ache of cracked ribs. He fought for equilibrium as he heard his nemesis gasp and gurgle in the throws of death. It was such a torment that he could not witness the grand event, so digging up his last ounce of mystic power, he sent his mind wandering. There, a few steps away, was Myles Ferguson, the joke of a knight, impervious to mental intrusion. Though, he didn't need the man's mind to see through his eyes. A passive psychic link allowed him all the access he needed to behold the final fate of the arrogant sage.

Mortimer was coughing up blood, with a sword through his chest. That shiny saber Myles liked to wave around boldly remained in the wicked wizard's gullet, assuring the man could not heal himself. The blade's anti-magic properties, coupled with Myles' own magic augmentation, assured that it would spell doom for even someone as powerful as Blythe the Bastard.

Strangely enough, Mortimer didn't seem to fight his fate, perhaps knowing it was futile, or grateful for a final end. Whatever the case, he knelt there, looking on as the blood poured from his pierced clavicle. When his body went limp and he pitched forward, Myles pushed his blade along with him, keeping it in place until Mortimer's death was complete.

When no signs of life remained within Mortimer's body, Myles pulled his sword free and wiped it off on the dead man's robe. He shoved the blade back into its sheath and marched over to Tobias, who decided he'd seen enough.

"You did well, lad," Myles said as Tobias' vision went black again.

Tobias said nothing in response, realizing how pointless any reply would be. He'd done nothing more than serve his self-interest, yet again. He had his revenge, and the satisfaction was fleeting. What would become of him now that his purpose was at an end?

The quest that had defined him for the past year was over. His wife was gone forever, and he was wanted for murder. He knew the fate of Guild members who committed such atrocities, and he wondered if even his father's status could spare him. To be honest, he didn't know if he wished to be saved. The goodness that lurked in the back of his suppressed consciousness cried for atonement, even as his heartless consciousness searched for a way out.

"Can you walk?" Myles asked, grabbing Tobias' hand.

Tobias nodded, and limped along with the knight, heading for an outer hallway. Both men were bruised and beaten. Their bodies had paid the full measure for victory.

* * *

It was well after dark as Ron Grimes sat with the Fergusons in the sheriff's office, drinking a toast. The bottle was an aged scotch that Myles had saved for years, and though Ron was not much for drinking he appreciated the occasional nip. After all he'd been through over the last few days, he felt he'd earned it.

"So, where are you two going from here?" Ron asked after downing his first shot.

"Back to the business," Myles replied. "I've still got a mining company to run, and there's a lot of work to do before we can refine another batch of uranium."

Ron slapped his hat down on the desk. "Now why would you go and do something like that?"

"For the same reason we made it in the first place," Myles replied, placing an arm across Nora's shoulders. "My lady and I are going to take a tour around the universes."

"Good luck with that," Ron said, reaching for the bottle to refill his glass. It wasn't the wisest thing to do, as he was already feeling tired, and the warming liquor made his eyelids heavy. Doliber had left him in charge for the moment, but there was only one prisoner in residence, and he was pretty harmless. It was time to kick back and relax. That's the least a deputy deserved.

As Ron downed his second drink, Nora said, "Perhaps it's best we reconsider our travel plans."

"What?" Myles asked emphatically. "But this is your dream. It's what we've been working toward all these years."

"I know, and you know I long for more civilized settings, but the risk is too great. If Blythe taught us anything it's that unforeseen elements can crop up, even under the most carefully laid of plans."

"But he's gone, and who else on this world could pose that sort of a threat?"

"You never know, and that's why we'd best leave it alone," Nora suggested. "My own vanity shall not endanger any world ever again."

Myles picked up the bottle and put it to his lips. "Are you sure you can stand to live in this world of savages?" he asked before taking a swig.

"Maybe if you use a glass," she quipped, slapping his belly as he finished swallowing.

"I shall endeavor to please," Myles replied, filling an empty glass. "Oh, how's the elf doing?" he added hastily, as the thought crossed his mind.

"Joella's doing okay," Ron replied, leaning back in the chair, teetering it on its back legs. "The sheriff and I had her checked out by Doctor Wilson, and he said she'll be just fine after a little rest. She's got my bed at the boarding house, sleeping off the bruises."

"I hope she's better soon," Myles mentioned.

"Same here," Ron said.

"So, when do you expect the sheriff to return?" Nora asked. "He promised us a teleport to Sacramento."

"Who knows," Ron said. "He's taking Tobias back to his daddy at the Guild. There's no telling how long that'll take? I'd say kick up your feet and enjoy the night. It's bound to be a long one."

* * *

Sheriff Doliber returned Tobias Sylvestri to his father's home. The renegade son was still bruised and blinded, as he had been after his final confrontation with Mortimer Blythe, so a group of medlocks were summoned to take him away for proper treatment.

Doliber stuck around after Tobias left, wishing to speak with the Guildmaster.

"I am grateful for the return of my son," the Guildmaster said, sounding bland as ever. "I only wish it were under better circumstances."

"I expect you to fill out one of those fancy Guild Warrants with the gold seal in the corner," Doliber mentioned with a touch of bitterness. He'd hated to hand his prisoner over the Guild, but he had no choice. Not only did they have special jurisdiction over their own members, but as a member, himself, he was obligated to work in their interests at times such as these. Still, he didn't have to like it.

"Of course," the Guildmaster said nonchalantly. "I already have one filled out for you." He opened a desk drawer and pulled out a piece of hefty paper with a golden infinity symbol stamped on the lower right hand corner, certifying the document's authenticity.

Doliber took the Warrant and read it, seeing everything to be in order. All of the ink was old, except for the date, which was fairly fresh. "You knew all along who I was chasing," he remarked.

"I'm sure you deduced that from the memories you stole from me," the Guildmaster said. "I was certain you would not heed my warnings, so I prepared accordingly."

"Lucky for you," Doliber answered, "for if I hadn't acted, we wouldn't be alive to talk about it."

"Oh, nonsense," the Guildmaster said dismissively. "Your actions, while adequate, were not above and beyond the full force of the Guild. Had you failed to act, we would have stopped Mortimer ourselves."

Doliber had heard such boasts before, yet he felt the words were empty. In all the years of the Guild's existence, they had done little to thwart worldly threats. They were more interested in personal introspection and perfecting their powers than actually doing anything. When the War Between the States had called, only a handful of warlocks had dared to defy the Guild's non-interference doctrine and helped either side. How many kings and tyrants continued to rule in foreign lands while the Guild sat idle? How many murderers and rapists roamed the streets of America, because no one of mystical training would stoop so low as to involve themselves in "civil" actions?

It was a disgrace how the Guild turned a blind eye to the wrongs of this world. Yet, there was an inkling of hope.

"It was you," Doliber mentioned, getting to the subject he'd been waiting to spring. "You're the one who talked to Tobias on the astral plain."

The Guildmaster nodded his head, looking pompously proud of himself. "As I said, I prepared accordingly. I was keeping a close eye on the situation, and did what I could to assist."

"Nice way to straddle the fence," Doliber mentioned, realizing how close the Guildmaster had come to taking a proactive stance. It was a step in the right direction, Doliber thought, though he doubted it would be repeated. The Guild would never permit anything overt, only minor manipulation from behind the scenes, and only when one of their own was involved.

Such a damn waste of power.

With the Guild's Warrant in hand, Doliber decided to depart, seeing no point in hanging around. Yet, as he turned to leave, the Guildmaster halted him.

"I must say, I was impressed with the way you handled yourself in this matter."

Doliber turned to look at the Guildmaster, and saw the man straight-faced. For a second, he'd though the compliment was made in jest, but clearly it was sincere. "Thank you," Doliber simply replied, feeling there was nothing else to say.

The Guildmaster would not leave it at that, and continued. "Many on the senior council share my assessment, that it is far time you took your Master's exam."

The offer was genuine. Doliber could see it in the Guildmaster's eyes, and for a fleeting second he felt prideful. Many warlocks served for decades before they earned the chance to qualify for the Master's examinations. He was barely thirty, and here was the opportunity being handed to *him*, of all people. However, the joy of the moment quickly faded, as Doliber questioned their motives. Why would the Guild wish to elevate someone like him to Master's status? Was it out of true admiration, or was there a darker agenda at play?

"Why" he finally asked.

"Your skill has never been in question," the Guildmaster responded. "You are a uniquely talented student, and it is time you had your chance to better yourself. I believe the examination process can do that."

The "process" was the thing, Doliber realized. What that would entail was anyone's guess, as none but a full-fledged Master knew the particulars. It was said to be a course of rigid mental discipline, to purge emotions and focus spellcasting skills. To become a Master, you had to conform, and it was something Sheriff Doliber was not prepared to do.

"No," he answered after brief consideration.

The Guildmaster smiled and folded his hands together. "Of course, that is your prerogative. If you wish to remain a Journeyman your whole life, no one can stop you. However, I would advise you take some time to consider it. The council's offer will remain open... for a while."

Doliber nodded slightly and headed out, walking down the long hallway leading to the front door. Stopping to pull on his boots and jacket, he couldn't wait to get back to Selwood, and the life he was building for himself there. It wasn't the most glamorous life, but it was his just the same.

Bonus Content
Episode Nine:
Date Night

Life was returning to normal for the law men of Selwood. After a few days of rest and regularity, Deputy Grimes was beginning to appreciate his new job. It wasn't all gunfights and busting heads. Most of it was just sitting around, and getting paid. How could he complain about that?

There was still a certain complication in his life, one he hoped to see remedied before too long. Legally, he was still married to an elf, and as much as that might sound appealing, Ron Grimes would like nothing better than to be free of her. It was all a sham, anyway, and he wasn't about to get any of the perks of married life, so the sooner he could cut her loose the better.

For the last few days, Joella Grimes-Talus had been resting at the Bormans' boarding house, following a life threatening thrashing. The bumps and bruises had turned out to be little more than superficial, but the doctor had ordered bed rest. It was high time she got back on her feet, and Ron decided to go fetch her.

Ron walked across town to the boarding house. Stepping into the weathered building, he was greeted by the elderly Mrs. Borman, who smiled and made a giggling noise, as if he were suddenly the butt of a joke. No doubt, word was spreading about his connection to Joella, so he'd have to get used to it. He couldn't deny the county gossips their vernacular sport.

Ron climbed the stairs and clomped down the hallway leading to the room at the far end. He rapped his knuckles against the last door on the right, and a moment later it swung open.

"It's about time," Joella said, standing in the doorway. "I've been stuck in his hostel for three days, and this is the first I've seen of you."

"It's just a boarding house, and you could've gotten out anytime you wanted."

"Not according to Doctor Wilson. He ordered me to stay put in this tiny little room."

Ron shook his head and smiled. Somehow he didn't see Joella as the order-following type. If she'd felt up to leaving, she would have. No, she'd chosen to stay put, and her protests were now part of her playful persona. Elves certainly had their quirks.

"Well? Are you here to free me at last?" Joella asked.

"I was just about to ask you the same question," Ron said, wondering how much longer their fake marriage had to last.

It was Joella's turn to smile. "Oh, yes, I'm sure you have a flock of women beating down your door, just waiting for the opportunity to wed you. Forgive me for standing in their way."

"Hey, that ain't fair!" Ron snapped. "You said we'd go our separate ways after you got rid of that no good cousin of your dead husband. We beat him, didn't we?"

"Don't count Mactus out too soon," Joella cautioned. "I'm sure he'll keep tabs on me for a few months, anyway. All the more reason you should have stopped by earlier. It would've looked nice for a husband to check in on his sick wife."

Ron realized how right she was, but didn't want to admit it. That pig-headed Mactus Sellius wasn't the sort to roll over, even after being shot in the arm. He was wealthy enough to pay for spies and God knows what else. A premature annulment of this marriage could give him the right to wed Joella against her wishes. Such was the twisted way of Elvish Clan Law.

Ron's thick beard couldn't hide the look of guilt on his face.

"Well, come on," Joella said, grabbing her brown jacket. "It's about time we had a proper night out. You can start making up for all this neglect."

Ron had mixed emotions about the idea, but decided to go along with it. She probably just wanted to torture him a little, as playful as she was. There was an elvish sense of humor he didn't quite understand, though he'd witnessed it firsthand on more than one occasion.

"Don't you have a nice dress?" Ron asked, thinking it odd that she always dressed like a man. That was odd for any lady, even an elvish one.

"Not unless you want to buy me one. Could you, dear?" she asked with exaggerated pleading.

Ron felt the fistful of dollars in his pocket, and wondered how much it would cost. Would it be worth a week's pay to make her look attractive?

"Say, you're on the sheriff's payroll, too," Ron remarked. "Why don't you spring for some new attire?"

"Hey, you're the one who wants me to dress up," Joella replied. "You want me in a dress, you pay for it. Otherwise, I'll wear what I please."

Ron rolled his eyes and led her down the hall. So much for that idea.

They walked out of the boarding house and headed back toward the middle of town. It was mid-afternoon, and a lot of people were walking around, doing business or just sight-seeing. Selwood was a growing trading hub in southern Nevada, so it was rarely quiet during daylight hours. As they walked, Ron could feel the people stare at him as Joella intertwined her fingers with his in an intimate grip. She had nice, long arms, which allowed her to hold his hand without it seeming too awkward.

"Are we gonna hang on to each other all day?" Ron asked.

"Just play along," Joella said, squeezing his hand. He wasn't sure what she was up to.

The Lucca Saloon was the biggest establishment in town, though Ron wasn't eager to drop in to see the obstinate barkeeper. He'd taken enough of the flippant elf's insults and cajoling during his previous visits, and he could only imagine what the uptight fellow would say when he brought his wife in for dinner. But that's exactly where Joella dragged him.

Ron was hoping for a small crowd, only to be disappointed. The saloon was unusually packed for a Thursday afternoon, with a lot of rough characters drinking and playing cards. There were a few families eating an early dinner as well, making for a curious cornucopia of patrons. Perhaps a packed room would allow them to blend in more easily. One could always hope.

Walking over to the bar counter, Ron and Joella took the only seats left in the place. It wasn't long before the proprietor of the establishment came over to see them.

"Oh, joy, it's Cousin Midge," Solen greeted him with mock enthusiasm.

"Right back at ya, Cousin Dandy," Ron replied, feeling a step higher on the status meter. At least the barkeeper wasn't calling him a Leprechaun anymore.

"So, what can I get for a happy couple such as yourselves?" Solen asked.

"What's on the menu?" Ron asked.

"Steak is always available, with assorted vegetables. Other than that, we..."

"Two steaks," Joella jumped in. "Well done. I don't want to see any of that red poking out while I'm cutting it. I get enough blood from my day job."

Solen turned his attention to Ron, looking oddly amused.

"Yeah, cook mine the same," Ron said, being less discriminating when it came to eating. He could take a steak any way, except raw.

"And to drink?" Solen asked, glancing out at the dining room, trying to keep tabs on the goings on.

"Bristling spring water," Joella replied.

"What, no wine?" Solen asked.

"No," Joella said, "and would it be so hard to free up a table? These seats at the bar aren't very comfortable."

"You should have made a reservation," Solen replied. "Not that I take reservations. It's first come, first serve, but I'm sure someone would be more than willing to move if you asked nicely."

With a curious wink, Solen moved off toward the far end of the bar. He scribbled their orders down on a note and handed it to a sultry-looking waitress who disappeared through a door that swung in and out after she brushed through it. Wafts of steam and smoke flowed out before the door finally settled back into a shut position.

"If we asked nicely?" Ron asked, wondering what that meant. Were they supposed to go around and pester the patrons for a table? That wouldn't do more than elicit a few laughs, if not start a fight. Solen was probably being his usual facetious self, taunting the dwarf and anyone connected to him. The arrogant little pointy would get his someday. Only, who'd be around to see it?

It wasn't the most comfortable setup, sitting on the tall stools without any backs, and Ron was feeling self-conscious beside his elvish bride. He could feel everyone staring at him, wondering about his perverse mating. He knew what they were thinking, because he would be thinking it in their place. *A dwarf and an elf? How Revolting!* There was no avoiding the truth; he was just as biased as anyone.

Solen came back with two tall glasses of fizzy water, which Ron scoffed at.

"Sorry, I assumed your lady ordered for both of you," Solen said, looking very amused.

"Go on, dear," Joella said. "It's good for you."

"What's the point of water that tickles your throat?" Ron asked, stirring the liquid with his finger.

Joella grabbed Ron's wrist and stopped his unsanitary treatment of the water.

"Your steaks may be a few minutes," Solen mentioned. "As you can see, we have quite a few patrons to serve tonight."

There was no reason for the obnoxious barkeeper to state the obvious—the place was clearly packed. The jibe was intended to add to Ron's discomfort, to let him know his agony would be prolonged.

This whole outing was a mistake.

"Maybe we should turn in," Ron told Joella, hoping she was feeling as uncomfortable as he was. "Seeing how you're still recovering."

"Oh, nonsense," Joella replied. "I'm feeling fine, really, but it's sweet that you care."

So much for being gentlemanly. Lowering his tone, Ron whispered, "Look, I don't want to sit here all conspicuous, with all these yahoos staring at us."

"We're married, Ron," she said, setting her hands upon his. "We'll have to get used to it."

Ron saw the barkeeper smirking at him from a few steps away, and knew better than to continue his protestation. They were in public, and they had to behave as a pair of newlyweds, for now. It was uncomfortable but necessary.

Joella reached over and gave Ron a peck on the cheek, which caused him to blush. The overt affection served to draw further attention from the full house. After a few moments, a scruffy character with polished spurs clomped over from the poker table and made a point to converse.

"Hey, midge, how's it going?" the man said, as he waved the bartender over.

"That's Deputy Grimes," Ron said, as the man ordered a shot of bourbon.

"Right, you're that new pint-size deputy." The cowboy downed his shot and motioned for a refill. "I seen you shot Lafayette there last month. Amazing you can handle a gun so good, what with those stubby little digits of yers."

"What's your problem, pal?"

"Nothin'," the man said, grabbing his refilled shot glass and holding it up. "Just wondering how a runt like you got so good, is all."

"You don't get good," Ron replied, feeling incensed. "You either are or you ain't."

"Well, it sure must impress the ladies," he said, turning his gaze to Joella. "Say, girl, whatcha doin' with a dirty little midge like him?"

Joella smiled at him and kept her voice calm. "Insult him again, and you'll be missing an ear."

The obnoxious cowboy started laughing, and then downed his second shot. "Hear that? The midge is so good he's got a whore to do his fighting."

Before the man could start laughing at his own words, Joella slid around on her stool and kicked him in the groin. As the man began to cringe from the blow, the elf pulled a knife from under her jacket and in a startlingly swift motion the blade lopped off part of the man's right ear.

Half the room stood up in response to the action, and it was no guess what was on their minds.

Joella hopped off her stool and retrieved the hunk of ear. "I'm no whore. He's my husband."

The statement convinced many of the patrons to sit down again, though a few remained standing, looking for a chance to move against her.

"How dare you behave so barbarically in my establishment!" Solen shrieked belatedly. "Deputy, arrest this trollop!"

"Excuse me?" Ron said, keep his eye on the handful of angry cowboys who remained on their feet. His hand dangled near his pistol, in case any of them was foolish enough to draw on Joella.

"You heard me, and you saw the whole thing," Solen snapped. "She assaulted this man."

"Self defense," Ron simply said, thinking he'd been about ready to pound the cowboy, himself.

"How was that self defense? The man was using words; simple, harmless words. This is my saloon, and I intend to press charges."

Several of the other cowboys shouted support, which helped to shift the situation to a less hazardous one. They no longer looked ready to draw, seeming more eager to have their friend's assailant locked away for trial.

"You're the sheriff's deputy," Solen said, slapping his hands down on the counter. "It's your duty and your job to arrest her, even if she's your wife."

There was nothing Ron could do, and getting out of there seemed the most prudent course of action, so he did it. Grabbing Joella by the arm, he yanked her forward, ordering her outside. She didn't put up a fight.

"And Deputy," Solen called as they neared the exit. "Don't worry about the steaks you ordered; I've already put them on your tab."

Tab? That was new. A week ago, Solen wouldn't have given him credit if he were rolling in gold dust. Attitudes were changing, if only slightly.

As they passed through the swinging doors, Joella squirmed free from his grasp. "Okay, enough of the show. Can we go home now?"

"You heard the barkeep. It's off to jail for you," Ron said, strangely amused by the situation. "I've gotta take you in."

"You most certainly are not!" Joella protested.

Ron cleared his throat and jerked his head back toward the saloon, where several of the cowboys were stepping out. The rough and tough men were keeping watchful eyes on the duo, looking to make sure the elf was taken to prison, and not let loose. Even if he wanted to, Ron couldn't take her back to the boarding house. She had to visit the sheriff's office.

The sun had set, and the dim twilight of dusk was settling upon the dusty streets of Selwood. It was a short walk up the block to the sheriff's office, and once there Ron marched Joella back to the holding cells.

"Don't you think we've taken this far enough?" Joella asked.

"Tell it to them," Ron said, motioning back toward the front room, where a pair of bold cowboys had followed them. Those guys weren't taking anything on faith.

Ron shoved Joella into the first empty cell and locked the door before going back to the office, where the two men stood. "Alright, boys, you can go now. The prisoner's secure."

"We want to see the sheriff," a clean-shaven cowboy said.

"Yeah, we'd like to hear it from him," the other said, brushing a hand over his neatly-trimmed beard.

Ron understood their concern, and he couldn't object.

Opening the top desk drawer, Ron found a glass orb and wiped his hands across it, activating a mystic summons.

"Say, what's that supposed to do?" the bearded cowboy asked.

Before Ron could reply, a flash of light appeared in the corner, and the figure of a man appeared. The tall, dark-haired Sheriff Doliber stepped forward and gave the men a courteous nod. "Gentlemen, how can I help you?" he asked.

"Is this here midge one of yer deputies?" the clean-shaven cowboy asked.

"He is at that," Doliber said, glancing back and forth from the dwarf and the cowboys. "Why?"

"His pointy-eared wife done stabbed one of our crew," the clean-shaven one answered. "We wants to make sure she gets charged, is all."

"Really? Joella Grimes-Talus stabbed a man? Is that so, Deputy Grimes?"

"Not quite," Ron said. "Their friend came up to us at the

saloon, started harassing us. Joella lopped off one of his ears when he wouldn't stop."

"I see," Doliber replied, glaring at the cowboys.

"Hey, wait just a darned minute," the bearded one said. "Joey didn't do nothing wrong. Sure, he may have thrown a few insults, but that shouldn't let the elf harlot off the hook. She attacked, he didn't."

"Yes, and she will be reprimanded for that, I assure you. However, it's pretty obvious your friend provoked her. He should know better than to pick fights with strangers in a bar. You never know who might be a deputy."

"What's that got to do with it?" the bearded man asked. "Your midge deputy isn't to blame."

"But my other deputy is," Doliber replied. "Deputy Grimes-Talus is also under my employ."

"What?" the clean-shaven cowboy asked. "Who ever heard of a lady law man?"

"And a pointy one to boot?" his comrade added.

The cowboys were looking angry, though they had enough sense not to challenge the warlock sheriff in his own office. Regardless, it wasn't a wise idea to let them stay mad, for various reasons.

"As you know, law officers are not above the law," Doliber continued. "I assure you, your friend will have his day in court, and Joella will have to explain her actions to a jury. In the meantime, I suggest you go on about your business."

The argument was over, and the cowboys had the good judgment to leave. They headed for the door, as Ron and Doliber relaxed, seeing they wouldn't need to use force.

As he yanked open the door, the bearded cowboy turned back and pointed an accusing finger back at the law men. "We'll be watching, Sheriff. Both of yuhs."

The door slammed shut, and Doliber turned his attention to the cells behind the office, where Joella waited. "What happened, really?" he asked her.

"He called me a whore," Joella said, gripping the bars tightly, as if she would bend them.

"That's all?" Doliber remarked.

"Excuse me?" Joella asked.

"There are lots of hard working girls in this town. Mistakes can be made."

"Not this time," Joella said through gritted teeth. "That man knew what he was doing, and was itching for a fight, only he didn't think I'd be the one to do the fighting."

"Exactly," Doliber said. "He was probably just a braggart, and you took it too personally."

"How exactly should I have taken it?"

"Sitting down," Doliber said. He shook his head and turned to look at Ron, who stayed sitting at the desk.

"Hey, I'd have shot him if he'd kept it up much longer," Ron exaggerated, feeling the need to defend Joella. She could be a nuisance, but she was growing on him.

"Deputies need to show more restraint," Doliber lectured, walking out of the cell block. "Get some rest, both of you. You'll be seeing the judge tomorrow."

* * *

There wasn't much to the courthouse in Selwood. Besides the sign hanging above the door, it didn't look much different than the rest of the buildings in town. Inside, you had room for about fifty spectators, along with the jury box and the stand. Trials were usually small affairs, which didn't garner much attention, though the case of Harold Lockward versus Joella Grimes-Talus drew a packed house.

The crowd wasn't the friendliest bunch; half of them being rowdy cattle men in support of Lockward. Sheriff Doliber had to call on trusted members of the community to help maintain order, as his two prime deputies were due to testify.

"Never seen such attention for a preliminary hearing," Henry Currant said, as he rubbed the pistol in his vest pocket.

"I don't even recognize half of these fellows," Doliber replied, realizing how many new faces were moving in lately. The large ranches north of town were drawing them in, creating a surge in population.

The grumble of the crowd silenced as Ron Grimes pushed his way into the courtroom, escorting Joella. Doliber's aides helped to keep the aisle clear, blocking a few surly individuals who sought to take a swing or spout a few slurs against the lady. The odd pair managed to reach their bench unharmed, and awaited the judge.

The door behind the bench swung open, and out stepped Judge Raymond. He was a portly fellow of advancing years, sporting faded robes and lamb chop sideburns. The redness of his nose and the dark circles under his eyes foretold of his after-hours activities, though he was never one to drink before five.

There was no doubt of the man's integrity, at least as far as Doliber was concerned. Judge Raymond had always done his best to uphold justice and follow judicial precedent. His mind was a wellspring of knowledge, and he judged every case with an even hand and honest scrutiny.

Yet, how he would see things in Joella's case was still uncertain. He might dismiss out of hand, or he could warrant a full trial by jury, depending on what was said this morning.

Judge Raymond beat his gavel and called the courtroom to order. Once things settled down, he allowed the lawyer representing the plaintiff to make a statement.

Lawrence Falkirk stroked a hand over his pointy, bald head and inhaled through his pronounced nose before leaping to his feet to speak. The cocky lawyer had a dozen years of service as Selwood's chief prosecutor, and so he seemed right at home as he began his tirade.

"Your Honor, this is an open and shut case in my opinion. The accused, Joella Grimes-Talus, assaulted my friend and client, the amiable Harold Waller Lockward. The accused did wantonly remove a large portion of Mr. Lockward's ear at the Lucca Saloon last evening in front of over two score witnesses! There is no doubt of her guilt, and therefore it is imperative that you empanel a jury immediately. To do anything less would be a travesty of justice."

Falkirk embellished his speech with demonstrative hand waving and a few quick glances at the spectators, who grinned back at his performance.

The judge prompted the lawyer to sit down, and asked for the defense to speak next. Judge Raymond assumed Ron was there to serve in the capacity of defensive counsel, though the dwarf was merely there as a bodyguard.

"I'll plead her case," Doliber said, clomping forward, pushing through the crowd.

"Sheriff, that is most unprecedented," Judge Raymond said, looking surprised.

"Perhaps, but she's my deputy, and I'll have my say."

The crowd began to grumble, as the sheriff's action clearly riled them.

"You may proceed," the judge said.

Doliber stood in front of the bench and made his statement. "To be fair, I haven't known Joella Grimes-Talus all that long, but in our short period of association she has served me as well as any man.   She has executed the duties of a sheriff's deputy with discretion, and I don't believe she would assault anyone without provocation.

"Now, the story I've been told, by both Joella and my other deputy, is that Harold Lockward accosted them at the saloon, and made slanderous remarks about Mrs. Grimes-Talus.   Lockward continued with his insults, even after Mrs. Grimes-Talus repeatedly asked him to cease, and she only took action when he refused to stop.

"I believe my deputy acted correctly, in an effort to maintain order.   If anything, Your Honor, Joella would be well within her rights to charge Mr. Lockward with disorderly conduct and public drunkenness; though I feel it would be in everyone's best interest to let this case drop altogether."

Doliber ended by taking a seat beside Joella at the defendant's table, and the courtroom blew up.   The angry crowd of cattlemen began screaming foul, and it took a furious pounding of the judge's gavel to silence them again.

Once order was restored, the judge decided to have his say.

"I am not one to procrastinate, so I'll make this brief.   There is clear wrongdoing on both sides, of that I'm certain.   In disputes such as these, it is common for the judiciary to work in conjunction with local law enforcement to discern a proper course of action. As the defendant in this case is an officer of the law, and Sheriff Doliber has spoken on her behalf, I believe it is wise to heed his words.   That said, we'll recess for fifteen minutes, so I might have a word in private with both the sheriff and Mr. Lockward."

As soon as the gavel fell, Doliber and Lockward were out of their seats and headed behind the stand, where they followed the judge into his chambers. Lockward's attorney rushed along behind them, seeking to stay on the case.

Most of the spectators remained, and it wasn't hard to overhear their boisterous conversations. Some were still optimistic that Joella would be sent to trial, for a jury would no doubt hang the elf whore for assaulting an honest drover. However, most were less than thrilled, and realized what would happen next. The sheriff's threat to charge Lockward paved the way for a deal, and none of the cattlemen much cared for the idea.

Ten minutes later, Judge Raymond emerged from his chambers, followed by Doliber, Lockward, and Falkirk. The men resumed their stations, and after tapping his gavel the judge called upon the prosecuting attorney to speak.

"Your honor, in light of the extenuating circumstances surrounding this case, Mr. Lockward has decided to drop the charges against Mrs. Grimes-Talus, with the stipulation that no charges shall be filed against Mr. Lockward for anything that may have occurred at the Lucca Saloon last night."

"Is the defense in agreement?" Judge Raymond asked.

Doliber nodded.

The judge called the hearing to an end, which resulted in an uproar of protest from the spectators. Though, after a minute of dissent, the crowd thinned, allowing Doliber and his deputies to depart without too much concern.

As they walked out on the street, a couple of burly fellows came up. Ron recognized them from last night; a pair of Lockward's poker buddies who'd followed them back to the jail. It was clear they were up to no good.

"Hey, Sheriff," the bearded one shouted in Doliber's face. "Don't think we're just gonna forget about what you done here today."

"Oh, really?" Doliber said, staring the man right in the eye. "What did I do, other than my job?"

"Your job," the surly fellow growled. "That involve lettin' pointies and midges walk all over honest cattlemen?"

"It involves making sure those honest cattlemen stay honest,"

Doliber said, turning to leave. He'd had enough of the provocative banter.

"I tell you right now, Sheriff," the bearded man continued shouting at Doliber's back.   "Folks ain't gonna stand for this. Pretty soon, you'll be out of a job!"

"Yeah, see you at the polls in two years," Doliber said, letting the irritation roll off his back. His job wasn't to be loved or make friends, but to uphold the law. He only hoped the voters would remember that.

As the trio continued to the sheriff's office, Ron leaned up against Joella and asked, "So, how was that for a first date?"

Joella glanced down at him, and then stared straight ahead as she replied. "I've had worse."

She didn't even crack a smile, but Ron couldn't keep from laughing.

Bonus Content
Flashback Short Story:
Grimes of War

The field was rank with black powder smoke. The stench of rotten sulfur stung at the nostrils of the warring factions. Blue coats and gray coats; each fighting for their own cause, knowing God was on their side to grant them victory in the grand campaign.

Ron Grimes still wasn't sure what to make of this conflict. He'd been drafted in '63, and assigned to the 2nd Pennsylvanian Infantry a month before Gettysburg. Since then, he'd seen a lot of things a young man ought not to witness. Still, he didn't let it weaken his resolve. He was pledged to serve, and his family honor demanded no less than his full measure of courage.

Cannon blasts echoed through the fields, as the sixteen inch iron balls flew into the Infantry's lines. As the cannonballs busted through, the Union dwarves paid a deadly price. The first two to be hit were tossed aside as mutilated wrecks, and three more had limbs removed. Ron kept marching with the remainder of his unit, praying silently that he wouldn't taste the sting of that fire.

The crack of rifles sounded next, as a volley of lead picked off a score of dwarves. The order was shouted to "Fire at will," and Ron unslung his shrunken Enfield rifle for the task. He wasted no time aiming at the line of Confederate soldiers who lurked within the haze. The white smoke of burned powder distorted his view, but Ron was still deadly accurate. He could see the blurry form of a man one hundred yards distant drop after he discharged his weapon.

Ron reached to his belt and grabbed his next powder charge.

Ripping the small packet open with his teeth, he poured the black grains down the bore of his rifled musket and set the empty paper on the muzzle. Grabbing a round ball from another belt pouch he set it in place and withdrew the ramrod to pack the wad and bullet into place. After twelve seconds, he was loaded once more, and raised the weapon to his shoulder for another aimed shot.

The dwarf division held their ground, even as their numbers continued to fall. They were front and center in the conflict, taking heavy casualties from the lead of the Confederacy. But they dared not retreat. If they withdrew now, and let their enemies march forward, it could spell doom for other units, which were maneuvering into a flanking position. So, the dwarves held their ground, as one by one the bullets sank into them.

Ron couldn't ignore the bodies piling up around him. To either side, his comrades were down, but he kept loading his musket and shooting back at the thousands of angry Rebels in front of him. If this were his day to die, he'd take as many of them with him as possible.

"Charge!"

The word was barely audible to Ron, as his ears rang from the gunfire, but the result of that command was much more obvious, as the line of Confederate infantry rushed forward through the white haze. The Union line was severely weakened, and a direct rush might break through. That couldn't happen, not here and now!

Ron affixed his bayonet, even as his captain shouted the order. He braced himself for the coming onslaught, ready to stab the charging enemy. The only thing that stood between the dwarves and a stampede of men were those ten inches of steel.

The Confederate troops appeared like a wall of flesh, with their own bayonets out in front. The full size men were screaming in savage rage as they ploughed into the line of dwarves, and it was quickly apparent who had the advantage. Even with an extension on their bayonet lugs, the shorter men couldn't hope to outmatch the tall humans in hand to hand combat.

The Confederate troops were tearing through the dwarf lines, stabbing and beating the shorter men into submission. Ron struggled to deflect two bayonets at once, knowing this was likely the end. He heard the screams of his fellows as the rebel bayonets tore into their bodies, even as he managed a lucky strike at the chest of one bearded foe in front of him.

Pulling his bayonet free from the stabbed man, Ron felt the world around him slow. The men and blades all crept along at a beleaguered pace, as he glanced back and forth at the combat. He thought it strange, until he spotted the Confederate officer aiming a pistol in his direction. Then, he understood. This was it, the final moment of his life.

A shot rang out, and the bloody field disappeared, replaced by a black haze of shut eyelids. He felt someone jabbing him in the side with the toe of a boot. "Come on, lad. Time to rise," a gravelly voice commanded.

Ron tossed aside his itchy blanket and looked up at the face of his uncle, the rough and tough Sergeant Brizban Grimes. The older man smiled from behind his heavy beard that was starting to turn gray, and the wrinkles around his temples revealed age contrary to the brightness of his eyes.

"Rough night?" Brizban asked.

"Nothing more than usual," Ron replied, sitting up. The dream had been haunting him for days, replaying those fateful events over and over again. How he'd managed to survive still amazed him.

"Well, it's still early, just a few minutes past dawn. Get your breakfast before we move out," Brizban ordered.

Ron rubbed his face and noticed a few days' growth of hair. It was itchy. He'd lost his shaving kit at the battle of Atlanta, and he'd had the misfortune of being sent out on patrol before he'd been able to find a replacement. He could borrow a razor from one of his colleagues, though he felt too embarrassed to admit his carelessness. Half the men in his outfit wore beards, so nobody would notice if he let his face grow a bit.

Stepping out of his tent, Ron was greeted by the hot and humid morning beyond what he deemed to be civilized. The mucky smell of rotting deadwood wafted in across the swamp, diminishing his appetite.

They'd been three days tromping through this wilderness, tracing down mail runners and mapping the supply lines, as the Union's Army of Tennessee besieged the city of Atlanta. This road through steamy marshland seemed like an improbable place for the Rebels to be hiding reinforcements, but the group of dwarves had been ordered this way, so here they were.

A sizzling noise caught Ron's attention as he sat down by the raging campfire. A wire stand was set above the flames, and a large skillet was filled with frying bacon strips, enough for each man to have several. A small sack of oats sat beside one of the sitting logs, and the chef was pouring water from his canteen into a tall pan. It would be a decent meal, likely the only one they'd have all day in this god-awful marsh.

The dwarves weren't much for conversation, and Ron couldn't blame them. This was a difficult situation, and there wasn't much that needed to be said. Though, his uncle had other things in mind, and as the bacon was dished out, the old Sergeant asked, "So, boys, what do you think we're doing out here?"

"Catching malaria," Private Winnow said before chomping down on a piece of the crispy bacon. He was young and precocious, but a true fighter at heart. Ron often wondered if he really was seventeen as he claimed, or a sight younger.

"No, no, I mean this war," Brizban clarified. "Why do you think we're down here?"

Nobody was eager to speak up. They were all fairly green as soldiers go, most of them having less than a year in the service. Other than Brizban, Ron was the senior-most member of their scouting party, so it fell upon him to give an answer.

"I've heard a lot of talk over the past year, and I've heard a lot of different explanations," Ron began. "Everybody's got their own opinion about why we're here, fighting the Secessionists. Some say it's to free the slaves, others think it's about preserving the Union. A few think it's just so a few businessmen can rape the South and get rich off it."

"What do you think?" Brizban asked, having heard this little speech before.

Ron lowered his eyes toward the fire, giving the impression he wasn't comfortable with the answer. "Maybe a bit of it all. I figure when it comes down to it, a bunch of people got sick of talking and decided it would be easier to kill each other."

It wasn't the most moralizing of speeches, and Ron didn't understand why his uncle felt inclined to plague the young recruits with such questions. What did he expect to get out of them? They were in the midst of war, and they'd all been drafted to fight an enemy most of them didn't understand, even as they recognized them as estranged kinsmen.

Nothing was so dangerous in the thick of battle than self-doubt, and someone had to say something to nip it in the bud.

"Killing's a dirty business," Brizban replied. "But sometimes it's something that needs to be done. There comes a time in this world when words aren't enough, and men have to settle their differences on the field of battle. The reasons for war are never simple, and they're rarely pinned down to one or two things. It's a whole bunch of stuff that piles up until the thin line of peace snaps in two. Then it takes a lot of blood to mend the divide."

Most of the dwarves nodded in agreement, showing their pride and confidence, though Ron couldn't shake the lingering doubts. This war had lost its shine for him a long time ago, and he no longer saw the point. As a draftee, he'd fought for honor and duty, not because he wanted to fight. There were plenty of good excuses for the conflict, but none of them were his concern, and it continued to bother him.

Right now, the best reason he had to fight was for his own survival, and that would have to do.

As the dwarves continued to eat their bacon, and the oats were put on to boil, a gray mist rolled in. The smoky stench of burning coal tickled at their nostrils, a familiar but overly strong scent. It was far too powerful to be from a single stove or foundry, and they weren't aware of any major settlements in this bog land. Something curious was coming their way.

"On your feet, boys," Brizban ordered, as the cloud of mist grew thicker. The acrid stench caused him to cough.

A hissing sound arose out of the fog, a menacing whisper like a dozen spitting vipers. The tone came and went in a circular pattern, as if something was spiraling around the campsite. It wasn't hard to assume it was some sort of attack.

A young private shouted in pain, then fell to the ground, thrashing and twitching nervously. Two more of the young recruits dropped in the same manner, as the hissing sounds continued to circle.

Ron reached down and grabbed his rifle, wondering if it could serve him at all against the mysterious assault. As he stood up, a small creature whipped past his ear, and he turned just in time to see the tiny features of the little humanoid figure. The charcoal-colored creature floated through the air without wings, propelled by a magical source, and brown fangs hung visibly out of its closed mouth. The being was known to Ron, but only through hushed rumors and childhood fairytales.

"Devil Mites!" Ron shouted after realizing what he'd seen.

"You sure?" someone asked.

"What's it look like?" another asked.

"Six inches tall, coal-black skin, red eyes, and needle fangs," Ron replied, as another darted past him. He may have been their next target, but his reflexes were good.

"Yep, sounds about right," Brizban said. "Must be a witch doctor in the Rebel ranks."

Such a ploy was new, and shouted of desperation. The God-fearing Southerners had never employed the services of the Voodooists before, as most saw it as akin to working with Lucifer. These were not the times for half-measures, and it was clear the Rebels were willing to use whatever means they could to preserve their Confederacy.

The wingless devils continued their attack, zipping around and biting several more dwarves, as Ron tried to spot them in the heavy fog. It was hard to see five feet away, and the dark demons were faster than a hummingbird. How had Ron been able to avoid their paralyzing bites? He knew his reflexes couldn't be that sharp, but somehow they didn't strike him down.

Then, suddenly, the hissing went away. No longer did the demonic assailants circle the camp of dwarves, and the sound of their magical flight dissipated into the distance. Their mission was complete, though the fog remained.

"Roll call," Brizban ordered. "How many of you are still on your feet?"

Other than Ron, only two other men replied; Private Corey Winnow and Corporal Patrick McLeish. That left nine dwarves on the ground.

Ron knelt down and found one of the fallen men. Checking the limp body, he found the dwarf was breathing steadily. Other than a bruised spot on the neck, there were no obvious signs of damage. Legend said the Devil Mite's bite was not lethal, that the foul demons would paralyze their prey, leaving them at the mercy of larger predators. Clearly, the old stories were true.

"This puts us in a tough spot," Brizban mentioned. "We can't take them all with us, but we can't very well leave them here for some Rebel patrol to find."

"If those Mites are working for the Rebs, they'll know right where to find us," Winnow said before stumbling into Ron. The fog wasn't letting up, and that told them the fight was hardly over. Someone or some *thing* else would be coming for them next, to finish the job the Mites had started.

A ghostly chuckle resounded out of the fog, a sultry, feminine tone. It was enough to set everyone's heart beating a tad faster, though what was to be done? The dwarves had no mystics among them, and were ill prepared for this sort of supernatural warfare.

"You can't escape yourselves," the lady's voice said. It was crystal clear, yet coming from every direction.

A stiff wind rushed through the campsite, and the dense fog cleared in seconds. The lingering haze remained over the sun, keeping a gloomy atmosphere on the scene, but at least there was clear visibility again. The dwarves looked around at each other, and at the unconscious bodies of their compatriots.

"Little men," the lady's voice sounded.

Ron heard the voice directly over his shoulder, and he turned around to see her, the dark haired lady with rosy skin and spindly limbs. She wasn't that tall, but she still stood well above Ron's head. Her slender body was cloaked in a blue gown that clung tightly to her waist; hardly the sort of person you'd expect to find in this dank wilderness.

"We're dwarves," Brizban answered, stepping up to the slim woman.

"What a relief," the lady said. "At first, I suspected the Yankees had resorted to using children for their army."

"What are you?" Brizban asked.

The lady smiled and knelt down to face the short man. "What I am is *who* I am," she said with an amused sound in her voice.

"Seems to me you're a witch," Ron said, feeling the weight of the musket in his hands. Something told him to use it, put an end to this strange woman before she could do anything worse, though his moral judgment prevented him from taking precipitous action.

"How very perceptive of you," the lady said, keeping her eyes fixated on Brizban. The whites shimmered like a mirror catching sunlight. "Your hearts are righteous, but your cause is unjust. Take to heart a truth of purpose."

Clasping her arms around Brizban's shoulders, the witch rolled her eyes, exposing pure, shimmering light for a split second. A powerful flash jutted out from them, and stung into Brizban's face. The dwarf's head was tossed back, as if a physical blow had snapped his chin, yet when the witch released his arms he regained equilibrium.

"Sergeant, you okay?" McLeish asked, looking bewildered. The young corporal moved to check on his commander, and Private Winnow moved to back him up.

"Arrêter!" the witch shouted, and froze the dwarves in mid-step. Rolling her eyes again, the light erupted from the shimmering sockets, and streaked into the faces of both men.

Ron had seen enough, and his moral mind felt justified to take action. Raising his rifle to his shoulder, he placed his aim right on the witch's heart, and pulled the trigger. The empty click echoed in his mind, and drew a sinister stare from his would-be target.

"Such rash behavior," the witch derided. "Did you really think I would allow your weapon to strike me?"

"It was worth a shot," Ron said, just before he lunged forward, stabbing his bayonet toward the witch. His aim was true, but his target was several steps away, and by the time he plunged the blade at her stomach, she had moved safely out of the way. However, Ron's bayonet did strike a fleshly target, the form of his uncle, Brizban! The dazed dwarf had been standing directly behind the witch, and took the sharpened blade directly in the chest.

Before Ron could fully realize what he'd done, he felt the butt of a musket hit him in the back, and several more blows slammed his head. He dropped to the ground as the blows continued, but a few sharp foreign words from the witch halted the assault. Ron was left dazed and bleeding, but alive.

Raising his head off the ground, Ron looked ahead to see his uncle lying on his back, gasping and clutching at his chest. The placement of the wound was deadly, and there wasn't much time.

"Imbecile," the witch chided, kneeling down beside Brizban. "It is hard to believe one so stubborn and quick to act could possess a righteous soul."

"What?" Ron asked, staggering to his feet, as his head pounded and tears welled up in his eyes.

"The Demon Mites can only strike those with injustice in their hearts; the greed, the envy, the infidelity of mortal life." The witch rubbed her hand over the bloody wound on Brizban's chest, and a shimmer of light sealed it. "For you to stand, untouched by their sting, then you must truly fall under divine protection. How strange."

Ron felt sick to his stomach, as he pondered the ramifications. "You say I'm some sort of Godly man?" He couldn't imagine it to be true. He hated church, and never really understood what it was all about.

"To hold such favor, a righteous man need not worship the divine, only serve it," the witch replied.

"And where does that place you?" Ron asked.

The witch raised an eyebrow most suspiciously. "Somewhere between dusk and dawn," she replied cryptically.

Brizban groaned and sat up with a little help from the witch, seeming no worse for wear. The blood stain remained on his shirt and blue jacket, but the flesh held no scar. He rubbed around at the healed wound, surprised to be so completely healed.

"Fear not, Sergeant. I won't allow you to die at the hands of this Yankee interloper," the witch said, giving Ron another nasty stare.

The statement sent Ron's mind reeling, as he fit another piece of the puzzle into place. It was obvious this witch was somehow connected to the Rebels, either as an active agent or just a freelance sympathizer. Yet, the truth of her purpose here remained unclear, until his uncle spoke.

"Thank you, ma'am. That's most appreciated," Brizban said with a slurred Southern accent.

Winnow and McLeish walked over to check on the sergeant, as Ron continued to work everything out. This witch was using some sort of mind control, a demonic possession that chilled him to the bone. What a horrible fate, to be turned against the Union in such a perverse manner. Was he next?

"Well, I'd say we've hung around here long enough," Brizban said, taking off his bloody jacket and tossing it to the ground. "Best we headed back to Atlanta, see if we can't break the siege in the South's favor."

"Hey, wait just a minute," Ron said, stepping forward, only to be halted by McLeish's bayonet.

"What about him?" McLeish asked, holding the bayonet under Ron's chin.

Brizban gave Ron a scrutinizing look and frowned. "Leave him."

"You sure?" McLeish asked, looking eager to kill.

"One misguided dwarf isn't going to turn the tide of this war. Besides, he's family, even if he is a damned Yankee at that."

"So are you, Uncle!" Ron protested.

McLeish set the Bayonet on Ron's neck, ready to slice him. "Say the word, Sergeant."

"Stand down, Corporal," Brizban snapped, then turned to Ron. "And you, don't think of provoking me further. I expect you'll wise up when this war is over, but until then you'd best steer clear of me."

With a wave of his hand, Brizban ordered his two remaining men to follow him, and they marched off with what little they had on them, leaving the rest of their gear with Ron and the unconscious men of the scouting party.

Ron could do nothing but watch them leave, feeling the evil stare of the witch upon his back.

"What now?" he asked, wondering what the witch had planned for him. "You gonna turn me like them, make me a good little Confederate zombie?"

The witch shouted some foreign curses and knelt down to face the small man. "You still don't understand. All that I've done has been for the defense of my homeland, the lives of my sisters. I saved your uncle's life, and still you remain blind? I am not your enemy."

"Could've fooled me," Ron said. "You're the one who attacked us in the first place."

The witch growled. "Your mind is closed, and I shall not open it." She stood up and spit on the ground beside the dwarf. "Your soul will ever seek justice, but it shall never find peace. That is my promise!"

A blinding flash of light left Ron staggering, and as the brightness faded and vision returned, he found himself alone in the clearing, the bodies of his unconscious comrades gone, along with all other signs of the camp. He was alone with the clothes on his back, trapped several days march inside this marsh wilderness. Even his musket was absent, leaving him with only the Remington revolver strapped to his hip for protection. He'd always preferred a long gun, but he'd have to make do.

It would be a hard march out of this swamp, but he was determined to make it. The siege of Atlanta could use an extra pair of hands, and once that vital goal was achieved, maybe he'd get a chance to return to this place with mystic reinforcements, and hunt down that vile witch who'd stolen his uncle's heart and soul.

If only fate could be so bold...

Bonus Content
Deleted Scene
:

The editing process for West of the Warlock brought a few alterations to the text, though rarely did we change the overall story. However, when we came to Episode 3, I had a short concluding scene written which we later decided could be cut, to help the story flow faster. It wasn't something that really contributed to anything later on in the tale, and it merely served as a brief epilogue to the scenes with the Sellius brothers.

* * *

At dawn, Gregory Sellius rode into Ravenna-West for some incidentals. A few gallons of whale oil, some fresh lamp wicks, and a few new books were top of the agenda. After a quick stop at the general store, he went to visit the High Minister and tell him about the duel.

"So, is he dead?" Ebenezer asked about Mactus.

"No," Gregory said with a frown. "The blasted midge couldn't shoot straight. He even had the nerve to blame my gun!"

"Oh, feel better, Gregory. You'll have your inheritance one of these days. Mactus is a deliberate man, who's bound to get himself shot sooner or later. If he doesn't wise up, you'll have his estate before too long, and perhaps even his wives, assuming they don't claim Widow's Rights on his killer."

Gregory nodded and felt his optimism returning. For so long he had lurked in his big brother's shadow, playing the dutiful kinsmen, all the while coveting the family fortune. It should all be his someday, and any opportunity to expedite the hand-over was welcomed. He knew his brother well, and did whatever he could to stir the pot. All he needed to do was stroke his brother's ego, and watch the man leap to his own demise.

It was a disgraceful plan, and one most would consider quite dishonorable, though such was the rite of passage for many an elvish clansman, even among Clan Talus.

Bonus Content
Afterword

West of the Warlock certainly took its good time getting onto the page. Where some of my previous novels have taken mere weeks to write (though the average is about 2-3 months), this one took me the better part of 5 months to get it to a final draft. Many factors contributed to the beleaguered pace, though the final result culminated in the exciting adventure you have in your hands right now.

The inspiration for this novel was a little short story called "A Dwarf at High Noon," which I wrote in summer 2010 during a writing contest. I sat down one Saturday afternoon and threw the short together, taking a vague concept I'd had for years about merging Sword & Sorcery Fantasy elements with the Wild West. The initial creation was a pretty traditional Western tale with just a few magical twists (and of course the dwarf). This formula turned out to be an original concept, and it got me high accolades in the contest. Judge comments such as "Freaking Brilliant," and "I'd love to read more of Boron Grimes' adventures," let me know I'd struck a winning chord.

Moving forward, I polished the 3,000 word short story and submitted it to a few Fantasy magazines, hoping to get some equally thrilling responses from the commercial marketplace. A couple of rejections later, I found myself wondering if the writing contest judging had been a fluke, but then I submitted it to Hall Brothers Entertainment for their Villainy anthology. The rest, as they say, is history. Phillip and A.C. recognized the brilliance of this unique little tale, and shortly thereafter they asked if I'd be interested in writing a much larger story based on the same characters. Of course, I was, and after some discussion we settled on an 8-part serial to run on their website, followed by a print release.

Writing the "Fantasy Western" didn't seem that hard, though it took me some time to get into it. I'd never written a novel-length Western before, and this story was very much a tale of the Wild West, with Fantasy elements added in. There were certain things I needed to work on, especially the setting and scenery, as well as some historical events that I ended up including. The imaginative stuff came easily enough, though.

The plot came in 3 different bursts of inspiration. My first concept for the book was "A mad wizard seeks to destroy the world, and Ron Grimes has to stop him." That eventually evolved into the whole Tobias Silvestri & Sage Mortimer Blythe storyline that really comes to a head as the final climax. However, as great as that main story was, I needed something more. That's where the "Marriage of Inconvenience" came into play.

Expanding beyond the events of "A Dwarf at High Noon," I thought, *wouldn't it be fun to have Ron get married to an elf?* As I considered the potential comedy and catastrophe of such a pairing, the Widows Rights plot device wove itself into being, and that formed the basis for the first major hunk of the book.

For the middle of the book, I needed a good bridge, something that would "one up" the wit of the mixed marriage, and make this a real action-packed adventure. That's when Wyatt Earp came to mind. I've always wanted to write something about the famous lawman, and this seemed like the perfect opportunity. I could write him into the story as an "alternate reality version," and the infamous "Earp Vendetta Ride" was the perfect thing to exploit. I spent a little time boning up on the real-world events, and then rewrote them in the Fantasy world. I don't think anyone else has ever written the Earps fighting werewolves, so that's another first!

By the time I was writing the final parts (adding in the Sci-Fi elements of alternate realities and futuristic technology) I knew I had to come up with a good title. Throughout the writing process, I'd been hard pressed to find a proper name for the book. Such temporary labels as "Dwarf at High Noon Novel," or "Boron

Grimes: Law Dwarf" just didn't cut it, but inspiration hit me as I was putting down the last few pages. Returning Sheriff Doliber to the Warlock Guild, I realized how much of a role wizards were playing in this story. Even though the main character is a dwarf, there are many pieces featuring the warlock sheriff and the warlock villain. So, "West of the Warlock" was born. It's accurate and sounds kind of classy in my opinion.

It was a real thrill to put the final touches on this work, and I'm sure this isn't the last we've seen from Ron Grimes and company. There are so many more stories waiting to be written in this magical universe, and who knows where we'll be going next.

About the Author

Martin T. Ingham is the author of various Science Fiction & Fantasy works, including *West of the Warlock*, *The Guns of Mars*, and *The Rogue Investigations*. His work has appeared in numerous print anthologies and online venues. Influenced by the greats of speculative fiction (Heinlein, Asimov, Herbert, etc...), he utilizes wit and wisdom to create stories for today's readers with his own unique voice.

When he isn't writing, Martin likes to dabble in numismatics, horology, antique auto restoration, and he likes to play with guns. He currently resides in his hometown of Robbinston, Maine, with his wife, Jenna, and their four children, Sylvia, Wyatt, Kathryn, and Lois.

Learn more about Martin's works at his website:
http://www.martiningham.com

www.ingramcontent.com/pod-product-compliance
Lightning Source LLC
Chambersburg PA
CBHW031344170626
46807CB00002B/815